THE MASTERS BALL

by

Anne-Marie Lacy

To Caroline, Happy Birthday
to ee wonderful girl,
with all my love,
Daddy &
December 18, 2013

Published in the United States

by

Indigo-Inc. Publishing

Madison, Alabama 35758

Dust jacket layout/design Bagwell Macy PR/Advertising

Damon Bagwell, Michael Gomez and Donna Pritchett

Interior layout/editing Larry and Jerry Pefferly

Preface and Dedication

This book is a work of fiction, and the individuals and events depicted herein are the fruit of the author's fertile imagination. That said, within these pages I have attempted to accurately depict one of my favorite rare and endangered species, the Foxhunting Southern Gentleman. My life has been enriched immeasurably by contact with this exotic creature, whose old-world charm and chivalry are unfortunately qualities of a dying breed.

The Foxhunting Southern Gentleman is a beguiling combination of hero and rogue, part reckless adventurer and part homespun woodsman. He is set apart from the typical modern man by his love and understanding of nature, and his gracious behavior towards animals and humans alike. So if my characters seem familiar to you, perhaps you are lucky enough to have encountered one of these unforgettable individuals yourself. And if you have, you will understand why I am dedicating this book to the foremost example I know of: my husband Allen Lacy.

CHAPTERS

CHAPTERS CONTINUED

CHAPTER I
A MISSING MASTER

Annabelle Farley, resplendent in a black satin gown with a small train, sat on a tiny gilt chair at a table in the Pierre Hotel's ballroom doing her best to look cool and sophisticated. Like a child at a birthday party, the forty-three year old southerner was thrilled to have been invited, for the first time, to the ninety-seventh annual Hunt Ball of the Masters of Foxhounds Association. She was also looking forward to hearing her friend, Edmund Evans, a Joint Master of Tennessee's Hill County Hounds, give his annual talk. She surveyed the crowd at the various tables, men looking regal in scarlet tails and women looking chic wearing black and white. Just minutes before, all had been summoned from their cocktails into the ballroom by the clarion call of a hunting horn. Edmund, a past president of the MFHA and that night's keynote speaker, was Annabelle's new crush. Handsome and fit at sixty-two, he had finally turned his attentions to her after years of exciting several of her friends into indiscretions. Edmund was well known for his prowess in chasing both foxes and women. Annabelle was totally sure that her husband, Nick, a newly minted Joint Master of the Hunt, had been chosen because of Edmund's attentions to her.

But where *was* Edmund? Annabelle scrutinized the room. Even though Hill County Hounds representatives were seated at the very back of the room, a situation Nick appeared to find irritating, she did not find Edmund in his seat of honor at the head table. "He's probably still in the bar", she thought, "charming some latecomers with his tall tales of life as a dashing horseman."

She had missed him at the cocktail hour, too, where she'd wanted to tell him about her recent adventure. New York City's weather in January was foul. It had snowed two feet the day before and the temperature had fallen to fifteen degrees, but Annabelle and her two best friends, Marguerite Robertson and Shelley Fitzpatrick, were not to be denied their visit and the party. Wasn't the MFHA Hunt Ball rich in pomp and tradition? Hadn't they blown their month's dividends and allowances on evening gowns from Yves Saint Laurent, Vera Wang, and Ralph Lauren? Hadn't they searched high and low for the perfect black and white gowns that were *de rigueur* so as not to clash with the scarlet splendor of the gentlemen? Annabelle looked across the table at Marguerite's generous cleavage above her black velvet—a bit much, she decided, but definitely interesting to the men. She smoothed the strapless top over her own small breasts and comforted herself that her gown was more fabulous than her wedding gown had been. She did notice, though, that Nick, who sat across from her looking as cool and confident in his scarlet as he had at their wedding fifteen years earlier, was nonetheless turning his attention to the area above Marguerite's waist.

"Has anyone seen Edmund?" she inquired of the table. Harold, Marguerite's husband, said he had seen Edmund walk off with Hunt member Randall Dodge who, though living in New York, often flew to Tennessee to foxhunt.

"Oh, I'd like to see him, too!" cried Annabelle. Randall's globe-trotting single life never failed to entertain her.

A young Master of the Crimson Valley Hounds in eastern Kentucky interrupted Annabelle's comment to continue his questions about Hill County's horsy playground.

"We have some 40,000 acres of contiguous land to hunt over," said Nick. "Edmund has been extremely successful in wooing our landowners."

"Are most of them female?" Annabelle looked up. Edmund's exploits had obviously crossed the state line.

"No," answered Nick, somewhat sourly. "If they were, we'd probably have 80,000 acres!"

Annabelle resisted saying something controversial, such as objecting to a proposed Wal-mart for the town of Guilford in Hill County's foxhunting territory. Instead, she asked for the second time, "Where on earth could Edmund be?" Already the salad course had been served.

"Why don't you go round him up?" Harold asked her, laughing, as Nick scowled.

"I will," she replied with the same determination that had earlier gotten her and her two friends to the Pierre from the Plaza after having been deserted by their husbands on the hotel's red carpeted steps.

Standing in the Plaza's warm lobby only moments before, the women had blessed New York for giving them a legitimate reason to be swathed in mink, a rare occurrence in their native Tennessee. Now, as the snow renewed its efforts, they were shivering in their furs and Annabelle secretly wished for the sultry south. The women had watched their husbands slog through the mess the few hundred yards to the Pierre while cheerily calling out to their wives, "The doorman will get ya'll a taxi!" Unfortunately, Annabelle and her friends were fifteenth in line.

Annabelle had caught a glimpse of a dejected looking man pulling up on a bicycle that towed a sort of lawn chair on wheels, the entire conveyance covered in heavy clear plastic that zipped around its frame. Against the objections of the Plaza's doorman, and despite the derisive snickers of the other tourists, Annabelle had looped the train of her dress over her arm, pulled back the plastic cover of the tiny rickshaw, and bade Shelley and Marguerite to hop into the contraption with her.

As she now swept from the ballroom in search of Edmund, she smiled as she remembered the three women in their beautiful gowns being jumbled up in the small compartment like clothes in an overstuffed hamper. Annabelle had to lay prone over the other two in a space that could accommodate a six year old comfortably, the three swaying and lurching as the bicyclist-driver tried to get his legs in gear. She had made a joke of it. "Trip to Masters' Ball turns tragic when rickshaw driver dies of heart attack—details at eleven."

But, the valiant charioteer, though panting, red in the face, and puffing loudly, got them to their destination. Even though the trip seemed like ten miles instead of one-quarter, he shook the snow from his cap and ushered them out of their cocoon to the amusement of the doorman, saying, "Here we are, ladies!" Annabelle smiled again, remembering her only thought at the time had been, "What if Edmund saw us?" He would never think her glamorous or sophisticated again if he witnessed her disheveled exit from behind the plastic curtain.

However, they never laid eyes on Edmund during the interval of drinks at the bar, nor when finding their way to the ballroom where they sat down carefully after having spent time rearranging their makeup and attire in the ladies' room. Now, as Annabelle took stock of her surroundings—all she knew about the hotel was its motto, "From this place hope beams", a statement devoutly wished—she found herself in a close encounter with the very man whom, apart from Edmund, she most wanted to see—Randall Dodge, the debonair bachelor New Yorker. She greeted him effusively and a little coyly, standing back so he might take in her designer gown and appreciate its effect. To her surprise, instead of the flattering comment she expected, he simply said, "Not now, Annabelle," and rushed off. Annabelle felt deflated, but comforted herself with the thought that Edmund would certainly react in a more positive manner.

More anxious than ever to locate him, she swallowed her pride, moved on, and finally found herself looking down over a balcony next to the grand marble staircase that led to the hotel's main lounge. It was deserted, except . . . Annabelle gasped in horror! Directly below her, alone at the foot of the staircase with his head and right arm at grossly unnatural angles, lay Edmund. The scarlet tails were spread behind him, one showing its paisley silk lining. Annabelle did the natural thing—she screamed bloody murder and rushed down the staircase, almost upending herself and breaking a heel of her beautiful Manolo sandals in her rush.

Within seconds of her scream, the hotel staff, Nick, Harold, and many of the assembled Masters ran like a well trained pack of hounds harkening to the call of a huntsman's horn. Annabelle was found on her knees with her face close to Edmund's, crying, "He's not breathing! Oh, why didn't I look for him earlier? I knew it wasn't like him to be late for his speech."

And so it was that the ninety-seventh Masters of Foxhounds Association Hunt Ball came to an abrupt and tragic end as Edmund Evans' death was validated by the diagnosis of Dr. Robert Wolfe, Master of New York's Farmingdale Hounds. "He must have tripped on the stairs," was his brilliant diagnosis. Annabelle, for once not enjoying the attention she was receiving, thought about how she had imagined Edmund chatting somewhere with members of his unofficial fan club, so involved in tale-telling that he had completely forgotten his official duties. Instead, he had fallen to his death.

Within minutes, representatives of the New York Police Department arrived on the scene, curiosity at its peak. They had never before been called to investigate the death of a man who was dressed in such bright sartorial splendor, seldom seen even in New York City.

Poor Annabelle—her wondrous night at the Masters' Ball was over before it had begun, along with her hoped-for romance with Edmund Evans. After answering questions by the police that included if she had noticed anyone in the area where Edmund had been found, Annabelle realized she had forgotten to mention her run-in with Randall Dodge. She decided the encounter was not worth mentioning as it had been near the entrance to the ballroom, and he was probably returning from the men's room. Annabelle sat shivering in her mink coat holding a hot rum toddy, Nick's arms around her shoulders. Her dark eyes filled with tears as she realized Edmund would never laugh with her over the rickshaw adventure, nor regale her with adventures of his own. With that thought she broke away from Nick and ran to grab her old friend's hand one last time.

CHAPTER II
THE END OF AN ERA

The picturesque hunt country straddling Hill and Guilford counties that is the domain of the Hill County Hounds is like a snapshot from America's past. The area is easily reached from Nashville by traveling south on I-65, but the age of the automobile appears to end there. Within a quarter-mile of the interstate lies a horseman's paradise of unpaved roads that connect vast tracts of the most beautiful hills and dales imaginable. The area is sparsely populated with farmhouses, many owned by those who enjoy foxhunting, and are flanked by horse barns and fenced pastures containing equine occupants.

In addition to Guilford's aesthetic qualities, the hills teem with southern foxhunters' twenty-first century quarry of choice, the coyote. When the fox population began to decrease rapidly in the early 1990's due to the encroachment of coyotes, many southern hunts responded by breeding hounds with increased speed and stamina to pursue the faster animal. In contrast to foxes, coyotes rely on their incredible speed to simply outrun a pack of hounds, quickly leaving a Hunt's territory if it isn't large enough.

As a fulltime resident of the county, Annabelle Farley could look out upon the Guilford countryside whenever she wanted. Today, from her window seat perch on the second floor of one of the more comfortable old farmhouses, Annabelle stared out at the landscape with an unhappy face. Almost a week had passed since Edmund's tragic death. In fact, a memorial service would be held that afternoon in his honor at the tiny Presbyterian Church he had occasionally attended.

A light snow was beginning to fall which normally would have delighted Annabelle. She loved few things as she loved the Guilford hunting country—the working farms with their cozy smoking chimneys, the rugged steep terrain. The change in seasons or even the weather brought a new beauty to admire, but this year the sadness and sense of loss she had experienced over the past several days clouded her enjoyment of the first snowfall of winter. She wondered what Hill County Hounds would do without its most dynamic Master.

She gazed across the wide front lawn to where her young horse, Samson, kicked and cavorted in the white flakes. She could not recall another time when his antics had failed to bring a smile to her lips, but today she merely sighed and looked past him toward the road while waiting for her friends to arrive with more condolences.

In addition to missing her friend and mentor, Annabelle could not shake the feeling of dissatisfaction she had each time she recalled the manner of his death. It was generally accepted that he had slipped and fallen while descending the staircase, breaking his neck at some point on the way down and striking his head when he came to rest on the marble floor. According to testimonies of doctors at the inquest in New York, either blow would have been sufficient to have caused his death.

It was not the technical, biological cause of Edmund's death that kept Annabelle awake at night, however. Even after questioning everyone in attendance at the Ball, the police were still not able to establish conclusively what Edmund's last movements had been. Where had he been going when he fell? Why had he been heading toward the bar when the crowd already halfway through dinner? Although she realized these were minor events in a life such as Edmund's, she felt a compelling desire to know more details of how he came to be lying at the foot of the staircase in the Pierre Hotel, even if the police seemed convinced he had simply lost his balance.

She had not seen Shelley and Marguerite since they had returned from New York and parted at the airport. Today, she had called and asked them to come by for coffee and a chat, both to add a little normal activity to the day and to see if they shared her unsatisfied curiosity about Edmund's last movements.

Marguerite was the first to arrive so pulled her green Range Rover past the walkway to leave room for Shelley. When she saw the vehicle enter the drive, Annabelle jumped up from her seat and was downstairs to open the door before Marguerite could ring the bell.

The two friends said nothing for a long moment. Finally Annabelle said, "This is all just too awful. I can't seem to snap out of it."

"Well, none of us can," said Marguerite, closing the heavy old door behind her as they made their way toward the kitchen. "I don't suppose things will settle down around here for quite some time. Edmund was a huge influence on this Hunt, and this *place*, even," she said, meaning Guilford. It was true that Edmund had begun thirty years earlier to fight against the proliferation of strip malls, and worked diligently to secure permission from landowners to hunt across their properties.

"I know," said Annabelle. "He was a huge influence on me. I just don't feel there's any closure by the way things were left."

Marguerite was pouring herself a cup of coffee. She looked up at Annabelle curiously. "Closure?" she asked quizzically.

"I just want to know what *really* happened to him—that night at the Ball, I mean. Why was he so late for dinner in the first place?" Annabelle shrugged her shoulders as she spoke, clearly dissatisfied with her own inability to see deeper into that fateful night.

"We'll never know those things," said Marguerite, sitting down with her cup. "He was probably just talking to someone, telling tall tales as usual, and forgot the time."

"But who was he talking to?" asked Annabelle. "That's what I mean. It makes me crazy that I just found him there and don't know what really happened."

"That's the second time you've used the phrase 'what really happened'," said Marguerite, now starting to smile at Annabelle in spite of the grimness of their topic.

At that moment, Shelley appeared at the back door. Annabelle rose quickly to let her in, gave her a long, hard hug, and took her Barbour coat and hat while Shelley and Marguerite exchanged greetings.

"Annabelle isn't sure that Edmund merely fell down those stairs," said Marguerite to Shelley, raising her perfectly plucked eyebrows in a look they both knew to mean, "Oh, no— here goes Annabelle."

"I did not say that!" Annabelle stated firmly as she returned to the kitchen table where both her friends were now seated. "I just want to understand exactly how it occurred, that's all." She looked back and forth at their skeptical faces. "Don't either of you think it's strange that he was mysteriously late for dinner, then was just lying in a heap at the bottom of the stairs?"

Shelley gave a big sigh. "No one has used words like 'strange' and 'mysterious' to describe what happened to him but *you*, my dear. Edmund was an older man and he slipped and fell down a staircase. A fall down that staircase would have killed a man much younger than him."

"Edmund was not young, but he was quite fit," said Annabelle, in hot defense of the deceased.

"Well," said Marguerite dryly, "surely you can't think someone at the Ball would have wanted to harm Edmund."

"I don't know exactly what I think at this point."

"Oh, no! Marguerite, did you hear that? Annabelle, what are you planning?" Shelley was shaking her head at her friend, her green eyes wide with concern.

"Let's just forget it," said Annabelle, who had no intention of doing so. She had seen her friends did not share her curiosity and skepticism regarding the true manner of Edmund's demise. She couldn't have articulated her reasons, and knew they could be a result of her desire to deny Edmund's untimely passing, but she couldn't reconcile herself to the idea that he was simply the victim of slick dress shoes on worn stair carpeting. Rather than worry or alert her friends that she might be up to something, Annabelle preferred to let the subject drop.

The three women continued to talk quietly while sipping coffee, entertained by the antics of Annabelle's two Jack Russell Terriers, Fitz and Floyd, who seemed to be among the few creatures in Guilford not mourning the death of Edmund Evans.

- -

The little church was uncomfortably crowded, certainly to the degree of violating fire and safety codes if there were any in the tiny town of Guilford. Although it was somewhat absurd to be having a memorial service for such a well known and popular figure in such a small place, Edmund's Last Will and Testament had specifically requested his official service be held there. It had doubtlessly amused the mischievous

Edmund to picture the church filled with famous personages packed like sardines, the less fortunate having to spill out onto the lawn, all having gathered in his honor. Many were weekend residents who owned newly built or restored houses called hunting boxes from which they rode to hounds or spent relaxing off time. Others were Masters of various Hunts from all over the world. Great Britain and France were well represented, as well as most of the fifty States.

Annabelle noticed on one side of the church's front, and conspicuously separate from the foxhunting crowd, were Edmund's children from various marriages along with their long-suffering mothers. None of Edmund's offspring hunted or even rode horses which she knew had been a source of mystification and sadness to him. He had always said they particularly disliked foxhunting as it was such an expensive sport and feared it could deplete their inheritance. They had very rarely appeared in Guilford, shunning Edmund's cozy hunting box in favor of his more lavish, less horsy properties in Nashville and Palm Beach. Annabelle watched as Edmund's latest ex-wife sobbed with theatrical abandon.

Despite the families' attitude towards foxhunting, the program was made up entirely of speakers from the horse world. John Swartzkof, former Olympic rider and trainer, and close friend of Edmund, would give the eulogy. Edmund's fellow Joint Master of the Hill County Hounds, Warren Fitzpatrick, would also speak, along with Edmund's lifelong friend, Samuel L. Harbison.

Annabelle surveyed the scene from a seat in the front row along with the other Hill County Masters and their wives. She recognized many of the attendees from the Masters' Ball, and others from the pages of foxhunting publications such as "Horse and Hound" and "Covertside." For a moment she felt elated at her good fortune in finding herself at the forefront of such august company, but recalled the occasion and felt that, somehow, VIP's didn't matter anymore. In fact, being among so many foxhunting celebrities wasn't half as entertaining without Edmund smiling at her from across the room, fully understanding her enjoyment.

To Annabelle, Edmund had been an ambassador of the glamorous sporting set who hunted and rode in exotic locales all over the world and, despite his impressive connections and busy social schedule had found time to encourage her in her own amateur riding attempts. She could recall numerous occasions when, discouraged by that day's riding lesson and disappointed in her own inability to cope with the fear that plagues many adult riders, she would have 'hung up her spurs' in defeat until she received a long distance phone call from Edmund who was hunting stag in France or quail in Spain. He always managed to put small setbacks into perspective, and found ways around the larger ones. He had always called her "Kiddo", and to a woman in her forties, that, alone, was reason to miss him.

The realization that all of his attention and encouragement were forever lost to her started a fresh flood of tears, by no means the first, but the most painful since Edmund's death. Through the streams, generously mixed with mascara, Annabelle gazed dully at the pulpit and the current speaker, Shelley's husband, Warren Fitzpatrick. Behind him John Swartzkof was preparing to speak, as was old Sam Harbison, another famous luminary of the foxhunting world who was of the same generation as Edmund.

As she looked down the row of those standing in the wings, what she saw next caused her to stop crying altogether and gasp, grabbing her husband's arm in terror and surprise. Standing next to old Sam was none other than Edmund Evans wearing evening scarlet and a white tie! He winked at her mischievously and held a finger to his lips.

CHAPTER III
IN MEMORIAM

Luckily for Annabelle, Nick appeared to assume her most recent gasp was an expression of sorrow rather than amazement, and patted her arm. Annabelle blinked her eyes once, then again, but the figure of Edmund Evans still smiled at her from the pulpit.

Annabelle thought to herself that years of overindulgences had finally caught up with her. She had read, in a cursory fashion, descriptions of what alcohol, nicotine, and other forms of chemical recreation could do to the brain, but had always been skeptical of their veracities. She had considered such reports poorly disguised sermons preached by the puritans of the medical community against some of life's more enjoyable vices. Now, she wished she had read them more closely. Perhaps there had been valuable information on how to react when one began seeing visions of dead friends in formal attire.

In her distress, Annabelle had not paid much attention to the opening lines of Sam Harbison's portion of the program. Edmund, however, seemed to be listening closely and, judging from his facial expression, wasn't too impressed with his old friend's version of their mutual past.

"I can remember teaching Edmund how to blow the hunting horn," said Sam in his slow southern Georgia drawl. "I believe he got real good at it after a few years because I let him in on all of my techniques." Edmund rolled his eyes and grimaced at Sam's self-serving reminiscing.

Sam continued, "I always loved Edmund Evans like a brother. That's why I gave him such fine hounds to help his pack along. Hell, I can remember when he said to me, "Sam, I want Hill County Hounds to be able to run coyotes like yours at Fairfield." I said, "Well, Edmund, you know I'll help you in any way I can . . ."

Annabelle almost laughed out loud. With his upper lip curled almost to his rather large nose, Edmund's face was a study in exasperation. He finally looked her way again and shook his head as if to say that Sam had certainly not been humbled by his friend's untimely passing.

As Sam slowly droned on, Annabelle recalled one of her past experiences with the legendary old foxhunter. She, Nick, and others from Hill County had been in Georgia hunting with Sam's Fairfield Hounds. Sam's pack was well known for its incredible speed and tenacity in pursuit of coyotes, and on this particular day they had "struck", or found, a coyote early in the afternoon, running it for over an hour.

The terrain at Fairfield was much flatter than Hill County's territory, so open that a horse could run at top speed for long distances without having to negotiate a single hill. Needless to say, both riders and horses had to be extremely fit to endure such a grueling workout. Nick's tireless thoroughbred, King, was a winning ex-steeplechaser that, in horsemen's terms, 'had no bottom'. If any run had ever tired him out completely, no one knew it but the horse itself. Annabelle's horse, Samson, on the other hand, though much younger than King, was half draft horse and half thoroughbred—a perfect combination for the steep, trappy country of Hill County, but a little heavy for Fairfield's flatlands. After an hour at a full gallop, he visibly began to tire.

Many riders had already pulled out and were enjoying a cold libation back at the horse trailers. Proud old Sam Harbison was, of course, among the few still in the game, leading the group on a big thoroughbred that ran as though a demon was on its tail. Actually, old Harbison being on its back produced much the same effect.

There had not been a moment to safely sip from her flask, but Annabelle was parched and ready to stop as the hounds ran on. She considered telling Nick she'd had more than enough when a riderless horse came galloping past them with loose reins, empty stirrups flapping. She looked back and saw a crumpled pile of scarlet lying facedown in the plowed field. She and Nick automatically pulled up their horses and yelled, "Rider down!" as is customary when someone experiences an involuntary dismount. To their surprise, instead of stopping or even slowing his horse, Sam Harbison merely stood in the stirrups, turned his head and shouted, "Is it the landowner?"

Nick and Annabelle looked down at their fallen fellow hunter, trying unsuccessfully to determine if he was lying on a patch of his own real estate, when someone in the group answered, "No, it isn't!" Sam, still standing in the stirrups yelled, "Then ride on! The hounds are running!", and disappeared after the pack.

Annabelle shook her head at the memory. "Sometimes foxhunting people simply go too far, like Edmund", thought Annabelle, looking between her fingers to see the apparition in scarlet still there and still casting irritated looks in Harbison's direction. In the pause between old Harbison's recollections and John Swartzkof's arrival at the lectern as chief eulogist, she unthinkingly raised her hand to try to get the ghost's attention. She felt her face flush crimson as Nick grabbed her arm and regarded her with shock and embarrassment. She quickly snatched her hand away and pretended to adjust her hat as though that had been her intention all along.

Rather than mention himself, John began his talk recalling tales from Edmund's colorful history, and that appeared to be more to the liking of the dear-departed. As the ghost of Edmund smiled broadly and fingered his white bowtie, John recalled his most recent hunt with Hill County as

Edmund's guest. It had been a cold Saturday morning in early December soon after the first frost had killed all of the green plants, leaving the floor of the forest stark and gray. Scenting conditions improve greatly once that change occurs because, until then, the scent of the chlorophyll in green plants interferes with the hounds' ability to pick up the scent of a fox or coyote. Hunting is best on damp, chilly days when the atmosphere is heavy and holds scent close to the ground.

John recalled he had ridden at Edmund's side that day. Annabelle, who was now watching Edmund's ghost for his reaction, saw him smile and nod as if he, too, had fond recollections of their last hunt together.

Initially, the two men had stayed with the main group of riders called the Field. Edmund was very tall and rode a 17-hand mare named Party Girl. As John said the horse's name the ghost looked at Annabelle and grinned broadly. Few of their friends knew the horse was her namesake.

John described how they'd trotted along, chatting with the females and passing the flask with the fellows, until they suddenly heard the sharp, high note of a hound that had found a coyote. In seconds, according to John, the rest of the pack responded by adding their voices to that of the lead, or strike, hound, harking to his find. As the Field sat deeper in their saddles and tightened their grips on the reins in preparation for a good gallop, Edmund turned to him and said, "Let's go this way. I have an idea."

While the rest of the crowd smiled, Annabelle rolled her eyes at Edmund's ghost and muttered, "I've heard that one myself", provoking another quizzical look from Nick and neighbors on the pew.

John told how they could hear the whole pack in full cry with the Huntsman blowing "Gone Away" on his horn in praise and encouragement. John's voice increased in volume as he related following Edmund through frosty trails and down slick slopes. Both knew when "Gone Away" sounded the hounds were running at full speed and not just slipping slowly along after the quarry.

The two foxhunters did their best to keep pace with the hounds whose music could be heard off to their right, so loud at times that it drowned out the sound of their horses' galloping hooves. They charged over one coop, then another, Edmund's big mare taking the three-foot jumps as if they were just cantering strides. The volume and emotion in John's voice sounded like a southern preacher as he described the sight of "... thirty hounds boiling out of the woods on our right, so close together Edmund could have covered them all with his scarlet coat!"

Then, he dramatically lowered his voice as if in awe of his own story. "Look there!" Edmund had said, pointing to the left with his hunt whip. John had turned his head just in time to see a bushy black tail disappear into the end of a hollow log, not fifty feet ahead of the hounds. "How on earth did you know we should be at this particular spot?" John remembered asking in amazement, for he had rarely witnessed a sight as thrilling as when the coyote had dashed into the safety of the log without a second to spare.

Annabelle watched, spellbound, as Edmund's ghost began to finish the story before John had a chance.

"It was Black Bart!" Edmund said loudly, with a note of triumph in his voice. "We've run that old coyote more times that I can remember! He always runs the same way, across the stream and down by the old grist mill ..."

Annabelle looked around at the other mourners, including Edmund's son and two daughters. Could it be that no one could hear Edmund, but her? No one else so much as glanced away from John as he wrapped up his speech with a sentimental remark addressed to the wily old coyote.

"Black Bart," he said. "If he could, I know Edmund would thank you for giving him so much great sport over the years. When your time comes, I know you two will hunt again on the other side. But in this world, your old friend has had his last run."

Annabelle felt fresh tears destroying her makeup. She hardly dared to look at the pulpit, but when she did she saw Edmund was still there, actually applauding his friend's story. He gave Annabelle a parting wink and then slowly disappeared.

CHAPTER IV
RETURN OF A SCOUNDREL

After the service, Annabelle, Nick, and other Hill County foxhunters gathered at the home of Marguerite and Harold Robertson. Marguerite was a fabulous hostess, and the Robertson's restored 1920's home was the perfect setting to showcase her considerable abilities. Annabelle felt confused and drained, and for once didn't notice Marguerite's latest interior decorations.

As she stood with her hunting friends exchanging condolences in remembering their fallen Master, Annabelle began to feel that Edmund's ghostly appearance at his own memorial service was a product of her overly stimulated imagination. Even though their relationship had never been more than a flirtatious friendship, she had dearly loved the man and now missed him in equal measure, so perhaps it was not so strange that she should pretend he was still present in Guilford. After all, she had always been creative, hadn't she? She sipped a second glass of red wine and tried to relax.

Meanwhile, Edmund Evans stories were being told everywhere. She overheard Charles Collins, the youngest Joint Master, telling someone about his older brother's reaction when he had joined the Hill County Hounds in the late 1980's. "That sounds fine, Charles," his brother had said, "but isn't Edmund Evans a bit of a scoundrel?" Annabelle laughed with the others and tried not to think about her recent vision. The group was already eyeing her in a concerned manner that implied they had noticed her unusual behavior during the memorial service. She determined not to mention her Edmund-sighting to anyone.

Despite the easy chatter, an underlying concern shared by many in the Hunt was the uncertain future of their foxhunting territory. The continued use of much of the famous 40,000 acres Edmund had assembled was by no means guaranteed now that he was no longer with them. Most of the landowners who were not hunters themselves had given the use of the land to him personally, rather than to the Hunt as a whole. Although the other Masters seemed to find discussing Edmund's business matters in very poor taste as he was so recently deceased, the Hunt's territory was an issue so vital to its survival that the rules of polite society gave way to serious talk.

With the recent addition of Nick Farley, the remaining Joint Masters were all extremely personable and friendly. But it had been Edmund Evans who had successfully wooed even the most reluctant landowners into allowing them to hunt across their properties. This was, in part, because he had been born and reared in the area, defining he was 'one of them' where no one 'from away' would ever be. It was also because, scoundrel or not, Edmund had possessed a powerful charm which he used with great skill in the Hunt's behalf.

The rumor that Edmund had been working on the creation of a perpetual land trust so that the territory in Guilford would always be available to the Hill County Hounds was now, with his unexpected passing, just that—a rumor and nothing more.

Annabelle listened to the worried Masters as they discussed the future of the Hunt—a Hunt without its guiding light. The talk depressed her as much as the service had, and she began to feel sad and at odds with the world again as she had almost continually done over the past few days. In fact, the only time she had felt any interest at all in her surroundings was when she had hallucinated during the memorial service. She sighed at her own silliness, and soon she discreetly signaled to Nick that she was ready to go home.

Whether it was alcohol-induced or a natural combination of grief and several sleepless nights, Annabelle went quickly to sleep that night. She awoke, however, around 2:00 a.m. The house was silent—even the terriers were sleeping, curled up against Annabelle's feet. She loved how completely dark the nights were in the country, and thinking of this, she snuggled closer to Nick and tried to go back to sleep.

Twenty, then thirty, minutes passed. Annabelle shifted and turned, trying to find the perfect position without disturbing the bed's other occupants. Finally, she decided she needed something—hot milk, perhaps? It would have to be chocolate—plain sounded too awful.

Annabelle made her way quietly down the back staircase to the kitchen. She hoped Fitz and Floyd would stay in bed, but they followed her every move as usual, tonight being no exception. "Shhh!" she told them, thinking Nick should be allowed some sleep even if the rest of the household were up and about. She flipped a switch that illuminated only part of the room, mainly to ensure that Nick would not be disturbed by a light on the lower floor of the rambling old house.

The Farley's weren't fond of sweets and desserts, preferring to get their daily allowance of sugar through the consumption of red wine and the occasional whiskey sour thrown in for good measure. Annabelle wasn't sure there *was* such a thing as chocolate in the house, but after some searching she was able to locate powdered cocoa and sugar left over from her Christmas cookie making as gifts for foxhunting friends during the holiday season—rum balls, of course.

She mixed the two in a cup with some milk and popped it into the microwave. She would have to be careful to open the door so the 'beep' wouldn't wake Nick. After about a minute, she opened the door and took out the steaming chocolate. She decided to check and see if the concoction needed more sugar, and put the cup to her lips. At that moment, she heard a familiar voice say, "Hey there, Kiddo." The cup and its contents went flying, spraying chocolate over Annabelle's bathrobe and landing on the floor between the two terriers which began happily licking up the small portion that Annabelle wasn't wearing.

"Honey?" she heard Nick call from upstairs, "You all right?"

"Yes, dear," she said vaguely, for she was weak with fright. "I just spilled my chocolate—not to worry."

"Good girl!" said Edmund. "We don't want Nick thinking you're any crazier than he must already. You made quite a spectacle of yourself at my memorial service today."

Annabelle turned to face Edmund who was seated at her kitchen table, long legs crossed comfortably. He still wore his scarlet attire, and was just as she had seen him at the church and at the foot of the stairs at the Pierre . . .

"Wha....what's this?" she asked, stuttering in shock. There was no way to communicate all that was going through her astonished mind.

Edmund smiled. "Aren't you glad to see me? You certainly have seemed to miss me."

Annabelle let the statement pass for the moment. "Aren't you dead?" she choked. "I can't believe I'm talking to a dead person! Oh, god, I always heard rumors about insanity in my family. Thank god Nick n-never wanted children . . ."

"Calm down, Annabelle. You're not losing your mind. I'm *here*. Actually, I've been with you since that night at the Pierre. I just didn't let you see me."

"Why not?" asked Annabelle, trying for the moment to accept the fact that she was talking to a figment of her imagination.

"Well, I didn't want to upset you, for one thing. And, I guess at first, I hoped it wouldn't be necessary."

"Necessary? Why is it necessary now?" Annabelle felt more foolish by the moment. Talking to ghosts, indeed! She rubbed at her rather bloodshot brown eyes.

"Because, someone killed me, Annabelle! I didn't just slip and fall down those stairs!"

"I knew it!" said Annabelle loudly, and then clapped her hand to her mouth. "I knew it!" she repeated in a whisper.

"You were murdered! Who did it? I'll kill him!" Annabelle seemed almost reconciled to Edmund's shade addressing her like old times.

"Annabelle, please, just listen to me. I need your help, and I need you to try to stay calm." Edmund's ghost sounded just as persuasive as Edmund, alive.

"How can I be calm when I'm talking to a *dead* person? I'm either going crazy or you're haunting me, and I find either of those two possibilities upsetting! I bet I'm just imagining you, anyway. You're a result of Marguerite's pate´ that disagreed with me."

"Me, a bit of undigested beef? No, my dear", Edmund wryly replied. "As you see, I'm not wearing chains like Marley, and you are much too pretty to be Scrooge. And, I can assure you I'm not here to teach you any moral lessons. Why don't you make another cup of chocolate and maybe that will relax you enough to listen to what I have to tell you."

"Well, the first cup must have been good," said Annabelle, glancing down at the terriers that had licked up every drop and were starting to fight over the cup. She quickly took it away from them and, as she did so, she remembered a comment Edmund had made earlier.

"What did you mean when you said you had been with me since last Saturday night?" she asked suspiciously.

"I meant just what I said. Not every minute, of course, but most of the time."

"So you've been sort of hanging around me, haunting me, for almost a week?"

"No," said Edmund. "I don't think it's haunting if you're not aware of my presence."

"Oh, so you're just some kind of ghostly stalker! Anyway, I'm still not sure I believe you. Or, believe *in* you."

Edmund uncrossed his legs and leaned forward conspiratorially. "Okay, maybe this will convince you. Remember when you were randomly selected for a security check at LaGuardia?"

"On the way home, you mean?" asked Annabelle, starting to feel a little uneasy.

"Yes, on the way back from New York."

"I remember being checked, yes," she answered warily.

Edmund smiled shyly. "Do you remember what the young man who checked your train case asked you?"

Annabelle remembered very well. At first she had been somewhat pleased to be selected for a pat-down if only because it meant she wouldn't have to stand in line any longer. She was led past the other travelers to a separate area and allowed to sit comfortably while a young male security guard opened her Louis Vuitton train case and checked it for explosive devices or contraband. Knowing she had neither, Annabelle proceeded to relax and people-watch.

"Ma'am?" the young man asked. Annabelle wasn't listening. *"Ma'am!"* asked the young man more loudly. He held up a giant canister which somewhat resembled an aqua-lung. "Can you tell me what this is, please?"

Annabelle gave the man a smirk. "It's hairspray."

"Thank you." He continued to rifle through the contents of the case. Annabelle sensed that he realized he had offended her and he attempted to engage her in friendly conversation. "Are you a professional makeup artist?" he asked with a smile, gesturing toward her case.

"No, I'm not," said Annabelle haughtily, turning her head away to discourage further questions regarding her various cosmetics.

Recalling this rather embarrassing little exchange, she looked wryly at Edmund. "I remember what he said."

"He asked if you were a professional . . ."

"I said I remember!" hissed Annabelle. "All right, I believe you. You've been with me all of the time. I hope you got a big laugh out of his stupid questions."

Annabelle felt she now must believe Edmund because one thing was for sure—she had definitely not shared that particular experience with anyone as it would have given them ammunition for teasing her.

Edmund smiled at her. "You should have just told him that it's not easy to be as fabulous as you are."

Annabelle preened, mollified somewhat by Edmund's compliment. Her second cup of chocolate was ready so she sat down with it in her hand and looked closely at Edmund, arisen from the dead, for the first time. "You know, I'm really glad you're back. Even if it does mean I'm crazy," said Annabelle happily.

"I'm not touching that comment," Edmund said with a grin. "Now, let me tell you what happened that night and why

I think it was done. Then, we've got to figure out how to prove it."

CHAPTER V
HUNTERSLEIGH

Naturally, Annabelle got very little sleep that night. In fact, she wandered around in a daze over the next week, which Nick and her friends attributed to extreme melancholy and sadness over Edmund's passing. Had Nick known that Edmund hadn't passed at all as far as Annabelle was concerned, he would have taken her straight to a psychiatrist. As for Annabelle, after about three days of ghostly visitations, she realized she was actually seeing more of Edmund 'dead' than when he had been in flesh and blood.

That night in her kitchen, Edmund had told Annabelle he knew who had killed him and thought he knew why. All of his life he'd heard stories about victims of violent crimes whose souls were unable to rest until their killers were brought to justice. He'd said, "Those stories are true. Looks like I'm here to stay until we solve my murder."

Luckily for Edmund, Annabelle had a mind that expanded easily to accommodate whatever experiences came her way. She figured this was undoubtedly one reason he had selected her as the beneficiary of his other-worldly attentions— that, and the fact he knew she would do anything in her power to help him when asked. This more than made up for her lack of ability as a serious sleuth. To underestimate her guts and determination, even if she was generally considered just an amusing airhead, was a serious mistake.

Annabelle began to get used to Edmund's spectral presence and took his word he needed her help very seriously. The problem of just how to go about providing it was something they hadn't quite yet worked out. Clearly, no one would believe her if she started making unsubstantiated accusations of murder against a well known and respected individual without some form of proof. She and Edmund had already shared many a chuckle discussing possible outcomes if such foolish measures were taken.

Edmund believed there were several pieces of incriminating evidence in existence, and he wanted Annabelle to get her hands on them. One was a faxed message the killer had sent him only days before their confrontation on the night of the Ball, implying Edmund would be sorry if he continued his current course of action. Although Edmund recognized the communication as a threat of sorts, he had not realized the sender was intending to kill him. Annabelle remembered it was not Edmund's nature to be dramatic or fearful. In hindsight, he wished he had been a little more wary. "Oh, well, 'c'est la vie'," he'd told her. "Or, 'c'est le mort', in this case!"

The problem was, Edmund couldn't remember exactly what he had done with the fax. He had been working on several items of business that day, some related to his personal investments and some involving the Hill County Hounds, so had consequently received more than one. At first, he'd told Annabelle he must have filed it somewhere, but she knew it would have been characteristic behavior if he had simply muttered a profane pronouncement regarding the sender's parentage and then tossed the ugly epistle into a trash can. Then, he seemed to remember setting it aside as a reminder in case he was ever tempted to forget what a low-down character this particular individual really was. But, where had he put it? Try as he might, Edmund could not recall. Annabelle had the cheek to suggest that a recent blow to the head might have affected his short term memory, and Edmund responded by vanishing abruptly. This form of leave taking disconcerted Annabelle. Edmund apparently used it as a means of chastisement when she said something he thought disrespectful, which was rather often.

On the Monday following Thursday's memorial service, Edmund joined Annabelle at lunch time. Hill County Hounds had not hunted that Saturday out of respect for Edmund's death, marking one week since the Masters' Ball. Nick had returned to work in Nashville after the quiet weekend, so Annabelle sat down with a large bowl of tomato soup to which she added basil, sour cream, and thick slices of avocado.

As Edmund appeared beside her, she looked up from her bowl and asked, "Is it my imagination, or do you particularly like to show up when I'm eating?"

Edmund smiled. "Well, it's a pleasure I can no longer enjoy except vicariously, and you do it with such gusto, my dear. I almost feel as if I can taste those delicious looking chunks of—what is that—avocado?" Edmund hovered over Annabelle's shoulder.

"Do you mind?" she asked sharply, and was about to make some reference to his post mortem manners when he sat down in his chair with a heavy sigh.

"I'm sorry," she said, immediately regretting her earlier tone. "It just makes me nervous when you float around like that."

She paused eating her meal and regarded Edmund closely for a moment. His black wool tuxedo trousers were losing their creases, and his once pristine white tie was looking grubby around its edges.

She spoke casually so as not to hurt his feelings again. "Are you going to be wearing that same outfit from now on?"

"So it appears," he said unsmilingly, daring her to comment further. Annabelle decided discretion was the better part of valor and went back to her soup.

After a moment he cleared his throat and said, "I was just thinking about that fax. There's really only one thing to do, you know."

"What's that?" asked Annabelle between spoonfuls.

"You've got to search my office at the house here in Guilford."

Annabelle set her spoon down with a clatter. "You mean break in? Why do I have to do it? As a ghost, you can just appear anywhere you want, can't you?"

"You won't have to break in, silly. I'll show you where I kept a key hidden. And being nothing but ectoplasm has its drawbacks. I can walk through walls, but I can't really grasp a material object."

Annabelle was silent for a moment as she digested this new information about the after-life. There were many questions she wanted to ask, but felt it was rude to be too inquisitive. Then she remembered he was asking her to break the law on his behalf and decided he owed her a few measly answers.

"So, where exactly do you go when I can't see you?" she asked.

Unfortunately for Annabelle, Edmund had realized she was extremely curious about his condition and was too naturally mischievous to simply answer her question without making a game of it.

"Where exactly do I go", he mused. "Wouldn't you love for me to tell you? Mostly, I'm just watching you!"

Annabelle reddened brightly, recalling the embarrassing amount of time she had spent in front of the mirror that morning while trying to decide if it was time for plastic surgery or, at least, Botox. She decided to satisfy her curiosity another time and abruptly changed the subject.

"Is anyone living at Huntersleigh? she asked.

"No," said Edmund, appearing pleased that the conversation was back on track. "It's shut up tight as a drum. My heirs aren't interested in the place so will probably sell it soon—all the more reason to get the fax tonight."

"Tonight?" Annabelle exclaimed.

"Doesn't Nick have a law firm meeting tonight?"

"Yes," answered Annabelle, a little unnerved. Here was more proof that Edmund was apparently listening to her and Nick, even when she couldn't see him.

"What about Tiller?" asked Annabelle, referring to Edmund's faithful jack-of-all-trades farm employee.

"Monday's his day off which is another reason that tonight's as good as any. Soon, they'll have someone clean the place out. The fax may already be in the waste can for all we know."

Annabelle nodded, knowing that Edmund's children and ex-wives were probably all expecting portions of his estate. Annabelle had to agree the house in Guilford with its accompanying 150 acres would be worth far too much to be overlooked by the greedy horde.

"You're sure you know where there's a key?" she asked.

"Yes, yes, of course. So, are we on?"

"We're on."

"Great. See you tonight." Edmund faded away slowly, like he always did when he was pleased with Annabelle. This time he let his smile remain for a few extra seconds, reminding his bemused friend of the Cheshire Cat, one of her favorite characters from *Through the Looking Glass*.

"Maybe I'll wake up one day and this will all be a dream like it was for Alice," she said to herself.

"No such luck, Kiddo," said a ghostly voice from somewhere in the room. Annabelle just shook her head and went back to her soup.

Around 9:30 that evening, Edmund reappeared. Annabelle had been anxiously waiting for him dressed in jeans, paddock boots, and a black sweater, an outfit she thought appropriate for sleuthing, not to mention slenderizing and flattering to her pale complexion.

"Where have you been?" she asked. "Nick will be home before too much longer."

"Oh, here and there," Edmund answered airily. "This ought not to take that long. We had to wait until it got quiet around Guilford."

"In case you haven't noticed, it gets quiet around Guilford at about six o'clock. That was three hours ago!"

"Oh, my sense of timing isn't what it used to be. Anyway, quit complaining and let's go."

Annabelle rolled her eyes. Dealing with the incorporeal was exasperating at times, but what could she do? After heaving a heavy sigh of resignation, she went out the back door to the garage where her Mercedes was parked. As she opened the driver's door, Edmund appeared in the passenger seat still looking very dapper in his scarlet despite a few smudges here and there.

Looking at Edmund's permanent formal wear revived Annabelle's curiosity about his rather singular situation, and she couldn't restrain herself from asking what she felt was an obvious question.

"Can't you just 'materialize' at the house?"

"Well, I could, but don't you think this is more fun?"

Annabelle agreed that it certainly was, and they drove the relatively short distance to Edmund's house in companionable silence. As they turned onto the long driveway to Edmund's hunting box, Annabelle asked where she should look for the hidden door key.

"Guess," stated Edmund with a grin. Annabelle assumed it was payback time for all of her nosy queries.

"Edmund, I really don't have time for games right now," said Annabelle impatiently. "I need to do what I have to do and get out of here."

"Oh, loosen up, Kiddo. Guess where the key is—you've looked right at it a hundred times."

For a moment, Annabelle tried to remember if Edmund had been this irritatingly smug when he was alive, but decided it was neither the place nor the time for such an inquiry. She dutifully looked around the property, a well known gathering spot for foxhunters over the past twenty-five years. A pang of regret and sadness swept over her as she remembered attending her first Hill County Hounds party there five years earlier.

On the Saturday of her first hunt with them, the after-hunt party had been hosted by Edmund at Huntersleigh. Annabelle would never forget her first glimpse of the place tucked back into a little grove of trees with one of Guilford's famous hills rising behind it. Although the house appeared deceptively small and cottage-like when viewed from its front, numerous additions over the years had added up to 4,000 square feet. Painted a warm cinnamon color with dark green trim, Huntersleigh looked warm and cozy even when the rest of the landscape was harsh and frozen.

"Guess where the key is," Edmund said again, interrupting Annabelle's momentary reverie.

"I don't know, Edmund. Just tell me and let's get the fax and get out of here."

"Under there!" said Edmund proudly, pointing to a resin figure of a Jack Russell Terrier near the front door. The figure was hind end only, made to appear the dog had dug his entire front half into the ground. It had fooled many of Huntersleigh's guests over the years who'd momentarily thought it was one of the live animals Edmund always kept about the place, but were now living at the Hill County Hounds kennel alongside the foxhounds.

"Oh, that's clever," said Annabelle as she lifted the half-terrier and put her hand on the front door key.

She trotted on tip toe up the stairs and across the porch with Edmund half floating and half walking behind her. The night was very cold and deathly quiet. Nick had always insisted she carry a flashlight in the car and now it had come in handy, although he probably never anticipated she would use it to sneak into a dead man's house accompanied by his ghost. She opened the screen and gave a quick look around to see that no one was near to disturb the silence, then fit the key into the lock. She felt the key turn and the door gave slightly as it opened, smiling with pleasant surprise that the mission was going smoothly, thus far. Edmund followed her inside and then went over to a keypad by the window.

"Alarm system," he explained, and began entering the code so the alarm wouldn't be tripped. To their dismay, his ghostly fingers slipped cleanly through the keypad and disappeared into the surface, much like the faux Jack Russell Terrier on the front lawn.

"Here, let me do it", said Annabelle, moving quickly in front of him. "Okay, what's the code?"

Edmund hesitated momentarily, and then said, "Try 64…68".

Annabelle keyed in the numbers. "All right, now let's look for the fax".

The interior of Huntersleigh lived up to the promise of comfort delineated so clearly by the outside of the house. The old wood floors shone, brightly polished between thick oriental rugs in varying hues of crimson. The sofas and chairs, though undoubtedly costly, had been gratefully used by many a tired foxhunter over the past twenty-five years and were now worn and inviting. The ceilings were low in most of the house, some of them showing their wide oak beams that added to the nest-like sense of coziness. The bar had always been fully stocked, and a fire always roared in the huge old fireplace in winter. There were six spare beds upstairs and plenty of fresh eggs and Bloody Mary mixes for Sunday mornings. In short, it was everything a tired foxhunter needed after a long, exciting day in the saddle, and Annabelle sighed to think that the glorious hospitality was no more.

Edmund led Annabelle through his library where every shelf was filled with books on hounds and hunting, then into his small office just beyond.

"I know I was here when I received that fax," said Edmund. "Look through the stack of papers, there."

Annabelle began flipping quickly through the pile of paperwork he had indicated, seeing nothing that looked like a message of any kind. She grabbed the waste can and dumped its contents onto the desk and was trying to flatten a wadded sheet of paper when she heard a sound like a cross between a car horn and the mating call of a bull moose. Annabelle instinctively clapped her hands over her ears.

"Edmund, the alarm! That must not have been the right code!" she hissed, horrified at the blaring sound tearing through the quiet winter night.

Edmund looked bewildered. "I must have given you the code for the house in Nashville," he said lamely, shaking his head.

"We're going to rouse the whole county!" cried Annabelle, growing more furious and frightened by the second. Then, she thought of something.

"Does this fax have a memory?"

"A what?" he replied blankly, plainly made uneasy by the continuing blare of the alarm.

"The fax machine! If it has a stored memory, we can print out a copy of the one the murderer sent you."

Without waiting for a reply, Annabelle went over to the machine and trained her flashlight on its many buttons and controls.

"How did you know that?" asked Edmund, whose grasp of technology was tenuous.

"A friend of mine went through a divorce awhile back. She said she'd read all of her husband's faxes from his lawyer that way."

"Hmm," said Edmund. Annabelle thought unkindly that he was probably wondering if any of his ex-wives had employed that technique.

In the meantime, the alarm continued its obnoxious, discordant complaints and made it difficult for Annabelle to concentrate. She cursed and began pushing buttons on the fax machine. It was a new model with a multitude of options, so she knew better than to ask Edmund how to access its memory. How like him to have purchased the very latest technology, but never bothered to learn how to use it! At last, a paper with 'test' printed on it began to eject from the top of the machine.

"Now we're getting somewhere!" said Annabelle triumphantly.

"Annabelle, there's someone coming!", Edmund whispered, as if in his fear for Annabelle's safety he'd forgotten that only she could hear him.

Annabelle hurriedly pushed another few buttons on the fax machine hoping desperately it would stop ejecting paper, then ran out of the office and into the library holding the flashlight. She was not sure where she intended to go, but sensed that it was imperative she not be found in Edmund's office. She was already halfway through the room when she realized she was running straight toward the barrel of a shotgun.

CHAPTER VI
HUNTERSLEIGH REVISITED

Annabelle gasped and threw her hands up, dropping the flashlight as she did so. Just then, she heard a familiar voice cry, "Annabelle! My, god! I might have shot you!"

To her immense relief, the voice belonged to Charles Collins, Edmund's closest hunting box neighbor and Joint Master. While Annabelle collapsed in a heap on a nearby sofa, Charles entered an alarm code—apparently the correct one as the hideous blaring stopped immediately—and turned on the lamp beside her. As she took several deep breaths in an attempt to regulate her heart rate, Annabelle thought how typical it was of Charles to come charging over like the Cavalry instead of calling the police like an ordinary person. Charles led the First Flight of foxhunters who rode at breakneck speed over jumps. He was well known for leaping first and asking questions later, so it was not hard to believe he would grab the nearest firearm and fearlessly confront a would-be burglar. Annabelle had already mustered a smile by the time he joined her on the couch.

"Annabelle, I don't know what to say. I'm so sorry I frightened you, but I thought you were a burglar. What the hell are you doing here, anyway?"

As Annabelle struggled to formulate a plausible answer, Edmund whispered in her ear, "Tell him you missed me so much that you thought it would make you feel better just to be here with your memories."

Annabelle shook her head, both to refuse Edmund's suggestion and to encourage him to keep quiet. "I had loaned Edmund an out-of-print foxhunting book of mine that I'd had a terrible time locating. I just wanted to retrieve it before anyone thought it was part of his estate."

"Why didn't you wait until daytime?" asked Charles, as if he did not really disbelieve Annabelle, but felt she had put them both in a dangerous situation and he needed an appropriate answer. Annabelle was tempted to ask him a few questions of her own, mostly regarding his knowledge of firearm safety, but decided she'd better play nice under the circumstances.

"Tell him you dreamed about me and couldn't go back to sleep without coming over here first," said Edmund, now beside Annabelle's other ear.

"Will you get lost!" said Annabelle sharply.

"Hmmph!" said Edmund.

"What? I'm only trying to help, Annabelle," said Charles in bewilderment.

"Oh, not you, Charles," said Annabelle, realizing he must think, like the rest of her friends, she was losing her mind.

"Nick is working late and I was bored at home, so I decided to come here to look for my book," she answered sweetly, thinking that having a reputation as an airhead had never come in so handy. "I'm sorry I caused you so much trouble. I just didn't think, I guess. What are you doing down here on a weeknight?" Annabelle attempted to turn the conversation away from her unexpected presence in Edmund's house and knew that Charles usually spent his time in Nashville during the week.

"I'm having company this weekend and I needed to do some things around my place to get ready," said Charles, visibly relaxing.

Annabelle wanted him to continue talking of other subjects. She looked around the library. "Boy, we've had some grand times here over the years," she said, hoping to distract him further.

"Yes, we sure have," he replied, standing and walking in the general direction of Edmund's office.

"Damn!" thought Annabelle, remembering the mess she had left on Edmund's desk and on the floor in front of the fax machine. She rose from the sofa and took Charles' arm. "Remember that morning I had to cook breakfast in the dark?" she asked, guiding him toward the kitchen.

Charles smiled, "Of course. I still wonder how Edmund was functioning around here without any light." Charles referred to an incident that had occurred several seasons before, one that was illustrative of Edmund's lack of ability to do anything himself.

Edmund had invited Annabelle and Nick over for Sunday breakfast and provided a grand assortment of uncooked foods—steak, eggs, grits, and bread for toast—but had needed Annabelle to prepare them. Edmund and Nick made a quick run to the hound kennel while she obligingly went into the kitchen to begin cooking. Unfortunately, she was unable to find a working light fixture. She tried switch after switch, of which there were many, but the kitchen remained in winter morning darkness.

Charles had also been invited to breakfast, and upon his arrival he and Annabelle had agreed there must be a problem with one of the breaker switches. When located, however, the breakers all proved to be in working order.

Finally, Charles decided to try simply replacing a light bulb. Annabelle didn't really expect any results because, surely, no one would allow *all* of the lights in the kitchen to just burn out one-by-one, but that was exactly the case. Edmund had simply done without light rather than replace a single bulb.

Charles and Annabelle had teased him about his indolence many times, to which he responded by smiling and shrugging his shoulders as if he didn't see anything so remarkable about his behavior.

"That was before he had Tiller," said Charles, referring to Edmund's hired man who had begun working for him a year or so before his death. "He was such a tremendous help to Edmund. Did I tell you I've asked him to work for me, now that Edmund is gone?"

Annabelle agreed that Tiller was a valuable employee. She breathed a sigh of relief as she followed Charles into the great-room, continuing to reminisce as they went.

"Just don't let this young buck lead you into my bedroom, Annabelle," said Edmund wryly. He seemed to be hovering somewhere around her left ear.

"Not everyone thinks like you!" Annabelle quipped aloud.

"Pardon?" asked Charles, and she saw, to her dismay, that he was looking back at her apparently thinking she had spoken to him.

"Oh, I just meant that you have a great memory for past events. You really should write some of this down."

Charles smiled broadly at the compliment.

"Why, thanks. Maybe I'll do that."

As Charles turned back to examining the house and recalled parties and dinners they had all attended there over the years, Annabelle waited until his back was to her and made an angry face toward her left side. She hoped this would indicate to Edmund that she had had enough of his interference for the moment. Then she tried to focus on Charles as he rambled on about various Hunt members who had over-served themselves at the buffet table, sometimes with humorous and memorable consequences.

It was a glorious setting for such excesses, but there was even more to appreciate when one was sober. Edmund had an incredible collection of antique books on tweedy topics. Along with early editions of the works that every foxhunting antiquarian has on hand, such as Siegfried Sassoon's *Memoirs of a Foxhunting Man* and Gordon Grand's *Silver Horn*, Edmund had some rare and unusual tomes such as the autobiography of Squire Osbaldeston, a nineteenth century rake, who could easily have been Edmund's role model.

"It would be such a shame if this fantastic library is sold piecemeal", said Charles. "Too bad none of Edmund's kids have an interest in foxhunting." Annabelle could imagine what Charles was thinking. He had been Edmund's heir-apparent in the eyes of the foxhunting world, but unfortunately not in the legal sense. Annabelle made sympathetic noises and tried to hide her anxiousness to be out of there.

However, a tour of Huntersleigh was certainly not complete without at least a cursory glance at Edmund's sporting art. Paintings of famous horses and hounds by even more famous artists such as Sir Alfred Munnings and Heywood Hardy adorned the walls, along with humorous sketches by John Leech and Cecil Aldin. There were scenes of steeple chasing, foxhunting, thoroughbred racing, polo—all immortalized by the best artists of the last two hundred years. This time, though, Annabelle was much too distracted to enjoy listening to Charles recite the history of each piece. Finally, when Annabelle thought she would die of frustration, he returned full circle to the library.

"Well, I need to be going, Annabelle," said Charles, at last.

"Oh, did you find your book?" he asked solicitously.

"Oh, yes. I have it right here," said Annabelle, holding up an old leather-bound volume. "Thanks so much for your

The Masters Ball

help. And, again, I'm so sorry you had to come over here. I just didn't think about the alarm."

"Oh, no problem—I'm just glad I didn't shoot you!" shaking his head at the thought.

Annabelle turned out the lights and she and Charles left the house. She locked the door and replaced the key beneath the faux half-terrier beside the porch.

"Crazy of Edmund to tell me where the key was and then not mention there was an alarm," said Annabelle, hoping Charles would infer Edmund had shared the information before his death instead of less than an hour ago.

"Oh, that's typical Edmund," Charles said with a sigh.

This time, Annabelle managed not to flinch when the voice in her ear loudly proclaimed Charles Collins to be the illegitimate son of a cur dog.

Annabelle drove home as quickly as she dared, hoping for the first time in her marriage that Nick would be really, really late. When she was about halfway there, Edmund appeared beside her in the passenger seat. His arms were crossed and his lower lip stuck out angrily. He said nothing for a few minutes and then sputtered, "I can't believe you told me to get lost!"

"Edmund," said Annabelle in a placating tone, "I couldn't think of what to say to him with you talking in my ear. I had to come up with something believable, and quickly. Can you believe Charles? Nothing untoward is going to happen to your art collection with him around!"

"Hmmph," Edmund said somewhat less angrily. Annabelle knew he couldn't help but be just a little amused by Charles' behavior, even though he had been cursing him only moments ago.

"Actually, I have to admit he appreciates my collection much more than my own children do, even if he did cause us to leave the fax." He stared moodily out of the window until they pulled into Annabelle's driveway. "Well, that was a big waste of time," said Edmund. He sounded depressed and was starting to de-materialize.

"Think so?" asked Annabelle, holding up the book she had taken from the library. As he watched, she opened it and pulled out several sheets of paper with a fax machine address at the top.

"Well done, Kiddo!" Edmund exclaimed, and Annabelle, herself, was surprised and pleased she had managed so well. "Well done!" he said again. "I didn't catch your sleight-of-hand. Amazing!" He smiled proudly at his friend, and then faded away slowly, leaving his smile to linger.

- -

It was again cold and silent a few nights later when two more visitors came to Huntersleigh, but they had their own key and knew the correct alarm code. They were quite a bit more calm and purposeful than Annabelle had been, because they knew exactly what they were looking for and where it ought to be.

The younger, smaller individual waited impatiently while the other one painstakingly entered the alarm code. Although inferior in age and size to his companion, he was clearly the leader of the two.

No alarm sounded this time. They quietly made their way through the library into Edmund's office where they turned on the small desk lamp.

The leader took one look at the pile of papers and the upturned waste can on Edmund's desk, then turned to his companion, "What the hell is this?" he asked in the unpleasant tone of one who doesn't like surprises.

"I don't know, boss. I ain't been here 'til now."

"I don't know who else has a key", said the other one, cowering humbly, despite his considerable advantage in both height and weight.

"Damn it to hell!" said the leader as he looked quickly through the pile of papers. Not finding what he sought, he turned to the fax machine. Unlike Edmund, he was well acquainted with the various features it boasted, including its electronic memory.

To his surprise and dismay, an error light was flashing on the display function. "Some idiot has screwed this up!" he said furiously. He pushed several buttons on the machine, and when there was no response, he cursed again. With a swipe of his arm he knocked the machine off of the desk and onto the tile floor.

"Son of a bitch!" he now addressed his companion. "If you weren't so stupid, I could have sent you after the damn thing and not had to wait and do it myself. I ought to . . ."

The minion backed quickly away to avoid a fate similar to that of the fax machine. "Oh, boss, don't worry. Maybe he threw it away as soon as he got it," he said with the air of one used to being blamed for anything that went wrong.

The two intruders left Huntersleigh without what they had sought and locked the door behind them. Soon the house was quiet and still again, just as if they had never been there.

CHAPTER VII
A DARING RESCUE

The next Saturday morning dawned cold, gray, and wet, typical of mid February in Tennessee. As miserable as those conditions were for the rest of humanity, Annabelle and the other foxhunters knew it was perfect weather to run a coyote. The heavy humidity would keep the scent close to the ground and the noses of the foxhounds.

This was the first time Hill County Hounds had hunted since Edmund's death. As Annabelle donned her silk long-johns for protection from the chill, she thought about how differently she would have felt on this day if Edmund had not remained in contact with her—for this was how she thought of his ghostly visitations. Used to them now, she felt that having Edmund all to herself dead was better than sharing him alive, even if he occasionally got on her nerves.

She tied her crisp white stock tie and put on her canary-colored wool vest, then temporarily covered herself with a rough brown coverall. The stock tie was a silk four-fold from Annabelle's favorite clothing store, Horse Country, located in the tiny town of Warrenton, Virginia. Horse Country is to well-dressed foxhunters as Neiman Marcus is to their other clothing needs. At today's Meet, the coverall would keep her clean while she saddled and bridled Samson, then she'd replace it with a black wool frock coat with the red and blue colors of the Hill County Hounds on the collar.

Annabelle and Nick walked together to the barn. Samson and King both nickered softly in greeting, and King paced anxiously in his stall. He knew it was a hunting day and was eager to carry Nick in swift pursuit of the hounds. Samson stood calmly munching his hay. Though he was happy to see

Annabelle, he was more interested in fortifying himself for the day's exertions.

The Farley's lived in Guilford on a fulltime basis. Nick, an attorney in Nashville, had obligingly agreed to commute after he had been made a Senior Partner in the firm. He had to travel around the country quite a bit, but was otherwise able to set his own schedule and could usually be in Guilford on hunting days. Now, to Annabelle's delight, their home was only a short haul by horse trailer to any of the Hunt's "fixtures", or locations, where the group would gather to begin a particular hunt. Sometimes, the Farley's were close enough to ride their horses to a Meet. Today, however, they would haul their horses by trailer as would the majority of the foxhunters.

The terrain they would ride would be very rugged and steep, exciting and challenging at a slow pace and thrilling at foxhunting speed. The First Flight would jump coops that are angled wooden panels resembling chicken coops measuring three to three and one-half feet high. Coops are built into wire fences to make a solid obstacle for horses to jump and are common in most foxhunting territories, but in Hill County there were often sharp, rocky descents for horses to negotiate with only a few strides for take off over a jump, as well as upon landing. It was not an activity for the faint-of-heart.

The rewards were there for Second Flight, too. Annabelle looked forward to the beauty of the countryside as well as its challenges. She knew that anyone skillful and hardy enough would not only get a 'buzz' from the ride, but would be rewarded by magnificent scenery. The working farms—some imposing, some tiny—resembled a scene from a nineteenth century Christmas card.

Upon arriving, the Farley's fell in behind other vans and horse trailers that were lined up to enter the Robertson's 160 acre farm, Gone Away. Everyone would mount up and gather on its gorgeous front lawn and, upon their return, Marguerite and Harold would host one of their famous hunt teas—a euphemism for a lavish dinner with an open bar.

Annabelle loved the hour or so before the start of the Meet when arriving horse trailers with their equine passengers parked alongside each other, riders hurrying hither-and-yon preparing themselves and their mounts for the hunt. In traditional theory, riders and horses are supposed to begin the hunt perfectly turned out with gleaming black riding boots, shiny manes and tails, and spotless tack. In reality, many hunters give their tack a last minute wipe-down just before saddling up. The same eleventh-hour grooming standard is sometimes applied to one's own attire, and today Harold Robertson came walking swiftly up to Annabelle with his white stock tie draped around his neck, stock pin in hand. He had a distinctly sheepish expression on his ruddy face.

"Can you help me?" he asked apologetically. Marguerite is busy getting ready for the party."

"Of course", said Annabelle, and began to expertly fold the starched cotton cloth into a perfect square knot while Harold obediently stood before her.

"The man has been hunting for fifteen years and still can't dress himself properly?" Edmund said in an amazed sounding voice. Annabelle was startled as he had been quiet all morning, but this time she controlled her verbal reaction.

"You know, Harold, you probably ought to learn to do this yourself, but it's really no big deal. I once had a friend who couldn't even change a light bulb," she said, while carefully inserting the little gold pin into the knot.

To her amusement she heard Edmund blow a raspberry in her left ear.

"Thanks so much, Annabelle," said Harold. "I promise I'll learn someday. By the way, do you know if they've selected a Committee Chairman for this year's Hunt Ball?"

The Hill County Hounds Hunt Ball, held at the end of each hunting season, was a fabulous catered affair that required a committee to put on and, of course, every committee needed a chairman. The position was always held by a female, frequently one of the Masters' wives. It was a highly coveted and sought after honor for many reasons, not the least of which because the chairman decided seating arrangements. The Masters themselves made the selection of a chairman, and Annabelle assumed Harold wanted her to put in a good word for Marguerite with Nick.

"I don't think they've chosen yet, Harold, so I'm really not sure. Do you think Marguerite would be interested? I know she'd do a great job."

"That would be great, Annabelle…" Harold continued to talk but Annabelle couldn't understand him due to the loud invectives that were being shouted at her from the spirit realm.

"I really can't believe these people! I'm not even cold in my grave and here they are, jockeying for social positions and asking for favors as though I was never even here!" Annabelle could tell Edmund was not only angry, but also his feelings were genuinely hurt. At first, she couldn't think of a way to be much comfort under the circumstances without sounding ridiculous in front of yet another friend, but then recalled a conversation she'd had with Marguerite the day before.

"Well, we'd better mount up. Aren't you and Marguerite having a Stirrup Cup in Edmund's honor before the hunt?"

"That's a little more like it," Edmund said, sounding somewhat mollified.

A Stirrup Cup was one of Annabelle's favorite hunting traditions. Small glasses of port are presented on a tray to the mounted hunters who drink them down and hand them back, empty. A toast usually accompanied the tradition, but this time there was a moment of silence for Edmund, instead. Annabelle looked slyly around, knowing he must still be close by and hoping he was pleased by the tribute.

The mounted riders gathered around the Huntsman and hounds where each Master made a brief announcement and wished all a day of good sport. The Huntsman then blew a short note on his horn and moved off with his hounds, encouraging them with his voice and horn to seek a coyote.

Annabelle proudly waved goodbye to Nick and he tipped his black velvet hunt cap in response, looking like a handsome country squire portrayed by Ralph Fiennes in his scarlet coat and white breeches, mounted on his prancing thoroughbred.

Annabelle rode over to the Second Flight group to ride with them. Riders in the hunt field are divided into groups based essentially on whether or not they wished to jump over fences or preferred to go through gates. Each Flight is led by a Field Master who controls the direction and speed, his responsibility being to place them where they are most likely to hear and see hounds working. Typically, the First Flight follows directly behind the Huntsman and hounds at whatever pace is set by the pack, and jumps coops rather than slowing to go through gates. The Second Flight makes use of gates and may travel more carefully.

As she patted Samson's silky neck, Annabelle wondered which Flight Edmund would be with that day. She remembered he had typically 'taken his own line' behind the hounds, but supposed he might decide to stay with her. She smiled at remembering, for once, not to ask him out loud.

Annabelle loved riding in Second Flight chiefly because its Field Master, her friend Shelley's husband Warren Fitzpatrick, was adept at keeping everyone within earshot and view of the hounds even though they chose not to jump. He was a veteran foxhunter who knew every inch of the country and was gifted with the rare talent of predicting how the game would likely run, so he was able to position his flight in a perfect spot to see the chase. Annabelle had had many a good day's sport following him.

This Saturday, in addition to the usual excitement of the hunt, Charles Collins had Richter Davenport as his houseguest. Richter was the Master and Huntsman of the Waterford Hounds, Hill County's closest neighboring Hunt. Like Charles, he was an aggressive rider. Annabelle realized he must have been the guest Charles was preparing for when he'd heard Edmund's house alarm and had come charging over with a shotgun. When the riders assembled, Charles announced that Richter had brought some of his best hounds to hunt with them. Her heart beat so loudly she could hear it. It promised to be an exciting day.

Annabelle watched closely as Richter and Charles galloped off behind the hounds. She trotted along behind Warren, happy to be out hunting and wondered if Edmund would materialize at any point during the hunt. As was customary, the Second Flight waited for the First Flight to go ahead of them before taking a different route Warren felt would allow the best sport.

His group moved at a walk or a trot up and down the Guilford hills for the first fifteen minutes, staying close behind the hounds as they ran this way and that, eagerly sniffing for a coyote. Suddenly, they heard the cry of a Hill County hound, followed quickly by the unfamiliar voice of one from the visiting pack. Then they all chimed in, loud and joyous, indicating they'd picked up the true scent of a coyote. Hill County's Huntsman, Billy Cox, blew two short notes and one long, a signal called "Gone Away", on his hunting horn, both to encourage his hounds and to alert the Field that the coyote had left the covert. The notes were high, clear, and true, and

Annabelle wondered, as always, how Billy had enough breath to blow so well while riding at a full gallop.

The First Flight took off directly behind the hounds. Annabelle watched the determined faces of the riders as they sat deeper in their saddles, preparing for a long hard run. Annabelle looked to Warren, waiting for him to lead them in the direction he thought best. After a moment's consideration, he took off at a gallop down a trail to the east of where the hounds were running. The path led to a steep hill, some three hundred yards long.

Edmund warned, "Here comes a 'slider', Kiddo!", and Annabelle knew that he had decided to stay with her, at least for the moment. She had been intimidated by the steepest slopes Edmund had teasingly called 'sliders' when she began hunting. Today, Annabelle sat back in the saddle, put her feet forward in the stirrups, and gave Samson a loose rein. He was as 'careful as a cat' in the hills, and she knew she could trust him to carry her safely to the bottom.

As much as Annabelle enjoyed riding with Warren's group which she firmly believed saw more actual hound work than anyone else, she often wished she could jump her horse over the wooden coops at a dead run. Annabelle had purchased Samson as a yearling and was now five years old and balanced enough to learn to jump. She had begun the fundamentals of teaching him to jump small obstacles in her riding ring, but she was a long way from having the confidence to jump him at a full gallop when hunting.

She gave the issue little thought, today. She was happy riding with Warren who kept her entertained and safe at the same time, but was distracted in trying to catch a glimpse of the visiting Master, Richter Davenport, who was famous for his haughty demeanor as well as a reckless riding style.

The hounds were running fast, their eager voices echoing off of the hills, clearly close on the heels of a coyote and never losing the scent or 'checking' for even an instant. Annabelle and the others rode hard to keep up with Warren, for today there were no shortcuts he could use to put them closer. The pack was running too fast.

After almost an hour with only the briefest of checks, many riders had pulled out as they or their horses were exhausted from running over the rough terrain. Then, very gradually, the voices of the hounds faded until they could be heard no more. Annabelle asked Warren what was happening as he carried a hand-held radio to keep in touch with the Huntsman and other Masters.

"Hounds have run out of the county," he said worriedly. "Those of us who still have enough horse left need to try and help gather them up."

Lost hounds were a serious problem. A good foxhound is the result of careful breeding and years of conscientious training, making it a very valuable animal. In addition, each hound is loved like family by the Huntsman and his Staff, and frequently by members of the Hunt, as well. Their safety is always the paramount concern. Annabelle kept expecting a comment from Edmund, but for once, none was forthcoming.

It was at that point Nick rode up, his horse in a sweaty lather and pulling eagerly at the bit. Nick tried to keep him still long enough to talk to Annabelle. Samson, glad for the respite, moved calmly to the side to allow Annabelle hand Nick her flask. He swallowed the port gratefully and said in a low voice, "I'm really worried about the hounds. That coyote has taken them clear out of Guilford County. I just wanted to let you know I'm going to take King back to the trailer and go look for them in the truck."

Annabelle nodded and was about to offer to go back with him when a familiar voice said into her ear, "Tell them there's not time for that, Kiddo! The coyote has led the hounds all the way to the interstate, and four of them are about to try to cross. He's got to ride hard right now through the old Post Office trail and stop them!"

Annabelle had no chance to explain to Nick how she came by that information, but in a breathless voice she told him what Edmund had said.

"Why do you think they're at the interstate, Annabelle?" Nick asked, his face expressing fear and dismay as she was describing a dangerous situation, both for the hounds and anyone who tried to rescue them.

"I just *know*, Nick!" she said, and abruptly whirled a startled Samson toward the trail Edmund had indicated. "I feel it in my bones!" she said, hoping that would be a sufficient explanation and that he would follow her without more questions if she turned and galloped away.

Her surprise tactic worked. Nick followed, more to protect her, she thought, than because he acknowledged she had correctly divined the location of the hounds. Samson moved so fast that Nick was surprised.

The couple tore down the mountain, going as fast as their horses could safely carry them on the slick, rocky path. In a moment they heard the constant hum of automobile traffic, and Annabelle knew they were close to the interstate.

"Oh, damn!" said Nick, hardly hesitating a second before kicking King forward down the bluff. Annabelle looked down at the frightening spectacle. Four hounds were in various locations on the busy interstate. One had made it safely to the median, but was unsure on its own in such unfamiliar surroundings so was scampering back and forth in wanting to rejoin the three remaining on the shoulder. As

Annabelle watched, horrified, one of the three attempted to cross the traffic to join the one on the median. It cleared the first lane of traffic, but when entering the second, a massive RV came within inches of its nose. The hound stopped and crouched on the asphalt, afraid to move in either direction.

Just then, Annabelle saw Nick reach the bottom of the bluff. She kicked her horse forward, suddenly realizing that if Nick was going to help the hounds, someone would have to hold King. Samson, whose favorite gait was usually 'whoa', seemed to sense Annabelle's panic and went quickly, but carefully, down the bluff. Nick had already hopped down from the saddle and was calling to the hounds that were still hesitating on the shoulder.

"Be careful, Annabelle," said Edmund. "There isn't much shoulder here."

Annabelle nodded as she jumped down from Samson and took the reins of both horses. As the traffic flew by only a few feet from them, she was grateful for Samson's natural calmness and for the fact that King, an ex-steeplechaser, was not concerned about motor vehicles. At first, not recognizing Nick's voice, the two hounds slinked away from him. Then, one hound, understanding the language and the smell of horses if not the individual voice, began to inch toward him.

"Give me a stirrup leather!" he cried to Annabelle, who snatched one off of King's saddle and threw it at his feet. Crouching down, he unfastened the buckle, eased the stirrup off and laid it on the ground. Nick continued to call to the hounds that had stopped on the shoulder and were watching him about twenty feet away.

"Come on, fella! Hoic! Hoic!" said Nick, borrowing words from a huntsman's vocabulary. To his relief, one hound crawled slowly to him with its belly almost on the ground. He grabbed it by the collar and put the stirrup leather through it so the hound had room to move, but was safely caught.

He then looked to the others. While he had been securing the first hound, another had found its way to the median. Nick apparently decided those two would have to wait, since he turned his attention to the hound that had remained on the shoulder. Now that its pack-mate was standing relatively quietly by and seemed to have suffered no ill effects, the hound decided to come obediently when Nick called and allowed the stirrup leather to be slipped through its collar. Nick then had two hounds on a stirrup leather, like fish on a string.

"Two down, two to go!" said Edmund breathlessly.

"He's pretty amazing with hounds, isn't he?" Annabelle asked in a murmur. Edmund chuckled, "Of, course! That's why I nominated him to be a Joint Master!"

Annabelle wanted to question Edmund about that statement as she had always believed his admiration for *her* had been the chief reason, but the problem of what to do about the hounds in the median had become urgent. She had already removed the other stirrup from its leather from King's saddle and held it out to Nick. "Here, you hold these two," he said. "I'll cross over and see if I can grab the others."

The two stranded foxhounds were weaving back and forth, contemplating trying their luck to cross the southbound lanes. Nick waited for a clear spot and ran across the road carrying the stirrup leather. The hounds were frightened by his rapid approach and both darted away from him to the edge of the grass, almost into the traffic.

Annabelle winced in apprehension, but didn't dare make a sound. However, Edmund, who knew all of the Hill County hounds by name, yelled "Here Fallon! Here boy! Here Sandman!"

Annabelle looked at Nick who appeared not to hear him, but she saw the hounds turn their heads sideways, listening and looking for the source of the well known voice.

Nick continued to move toward the median, crouching low, making himself as small and unthreatening as possible. He called softly to them, "Hoic, hoic, *here.*" After a couple of breathtaking moments, and right when Annabelle thought they might take off onto the highway with even Edmund being silent, the two hounds came to Nick with heads low and tails wagging cautiously. Without further ado, he slipped the stirrup leather through their collars and led them across the road to safety.

"Good job, Kiddo!" said a pleased voice in Annabelle's ear. "I'm proud of you both. I really am."

CHAPTER VIII
AN INVITATION

The foxhunters at the Robertson's Hunt Tea were abuzz with stories of Nick's heroic hound rescue. Annabelle, who normally loved the limelight, minimized her own role in the drama because she could have never explained how she uncannily knew the hounds had been in danger and exactly where to find them. She felt sure that as soon as Nick had a moment to think, he would be asking her, himself. She decided to ask Edmund to come up with a satisfactory explanation sometime in the next few hours.

In the meantime, she was enjoying hearing Nick praised by all. In reality, only a man who had handled hounds all of his life, like Nick Farley, could have successfully caught and held the frightened animals, even if the information about their whereabouts was provided via ghostly intervention. Annabelle was proud of Nick and happy she had helped (along with Edmund) save the precious hounds. She flitted about at the party, making frequent trips to the bar for more wine and tasting the delicious hors d'oeuvres Marguerite had strategically placed around the house.

Dinner was served buffet style offering beef stroganoff made with tenderloin, mushrooms, and sour cream atop buttery egg noodles, a salad of fresh field greens sprinkled liberally with goat cheese and pepper, fresh steamed asparagus, and an assortment of miniature pies for dessert—chocolate, chess, and key lime—that rounded out the menu.

Annabelle relished the Saturday parties held after foxhunting almost as much as hunting itself. In her opinion, there was nothing more pleasing after a day of riding than the gathering of tired, happy, mud-splattered friends by a warm fireside accompanied by plenty of good food and drinks. She spied Edmund hovering around and listening to the tales told by riders from the three different Flights. She knew he was hearing accounts of great daring-do, often more imagined than real, and having a good chuckle. Several hunters had fallen off of their horses at some point, none badly hurt. They were surrounded by concerned compatriots who wanted to sympathize with their bruises and to hear either the gory details of their dismounts, or snicker at the braggadocio that accompanied 'not my fault'.

Today's opinion was that the four rescued hounds had been hot on the scent of a coyote that had led them to the interstate and had successfully dashed across to safety. One of the First Flight riders had been the first to see the coyote earlier in the run and, as such, had the honor of shouting "Tally-ho!" to alert the Huntsman and Masters that the chased game had been viewed. Annabelle heard this tale recounted as she drifted from conversation to conversation, Edmund at her heels, loudly confirming or denying the veracity of each story in her ear.

As she waited in line at the bar, Annabelle glanced around to see visiting Master Richter Davenport in a quiet corner talking with Charles, his host, and Felicia Blackwell, one of Hill County's oldest and most venerated members, who was known affectionately to one and all as "Miss Felicia". His face and manner were very serious, unlike most of the other party guests she observed who were smiling and laughing. Annabelle continued to watch Davenport through lowered eyelids and thought he would have been a very handsome man with his dark hair and blue eyes if his expression wasn't so cold and arrogant.

"I see you're checking out the young Master," said Edmund, with a sneer in his voice. "God, but you're fickle! I haven't even been dead two weeks…"

Annabelle, who had just worked her way through the line to the crowded bar, couldn't afford to reply so she just asked the bartender to refill her wine glass. Edmund continued to discuss Richter Davenport.

"I've known that young man for most of his life", said Edmund. "He's a great Huntsman and an incredibly bold rider. He's definitely not a people-person, however. He's managed to alienate quite a few of the Waterford members and even more of their landowners since becoming Master a couple of years ago."

Annabelle, with Edmund in tow, watched as Richter and Miss Felicia put their heads together in an intense discussion until Charles, with drink in hand, joined them. Making up her mind not to forego hearing Miss Felicia's views on Nick's recent exploits despite Richter's attempt to monopolize her, Annabelle approached the small group. She also thought it would be amusing to see how Edmund reacted in close proximity to a prospective rival.

Felicia Blackwell was well into her seventies and had hunted with Hill County since its beginnings in the 1930's. Her father, Tennent Blackwell, had been one of the Hunt's three founding members, and Felicia was still among the largest landowners in Guilford. Her homestead, Blackwood Farm, was only one of her several hunt country properties. Miss Felicia was still a bold horsewoman despite her grand age. She had made the transition from riding sidesaddle as a child to riding astride as an adult so successfully that she won many a point-to-point race as a young woman. Annabelle adored her and frequently wished aloud she had been blessed with even a fraction of the older woman's riding ability. She rarely missed an opportunity to hear Miss Felicia's perspective on a day's hunting.

"Well, Annabelle," said Felicia heartily, smiling from ear to ear. "I understand your husband is quite the hero of the day.

Do you know Richter Davenport, Master of the Waterford Hounds? He's here visiting our Charles."

Annabelle shook hands with Davenport who looked rather bored and irritated by the interruption. It was apparent from his reaction that Edmund need not be jealous on his account. Felicia loudly continued her praise of Nick Farley. "You know, Annabelle, one of the hounds Nick saved was Fallon who won the Virginia Hound Show for us last year."

"I'm the one that told you where to look for the hounds or they would have been killed in the traffic," said Edmund petulantly. "I hope you realize that Nick is only a hero because of me."

Annabelle decided she had to find a way to reply.

"Yes, it was a good thing we were there. And Nick is so good with hounds. I believe that's one reason Edmund Evans proposed him for Joint Mastership. At least that's what he told me."

"Touché, Kiddo!" said Edmund with a sheepish smile on his ghostly face. In Annabelle's opinion, Edmund's willingness to admit when he was bested was one of his more admirable qualities.

Charles added his commendation to Felicia's, adding that the other Masters were grateful to Nick for his timely intervention. Aside from her defense of her husband's talents to Edmund, it was clear to Annabelle that Hill County collectively assumed Nick's skill as a foxhunter had led him to the hounds and that she had merely followed him. Unfortunately, she knew Nick's natural generosity would make him want to extend the credit to her unless she specifically asked him not to mention her vital contribution. She decided to excuse herself from the group to find Nick before he publicly branded her a 'hound psychic'.

68

Just as she opened her mouth to speak, Charles patted her arm and said with a twinkle in his eye, "You never know where these Farley's will turn up. This one gave me a hell of a scare earlier in the week."

Annabelle froze, realizing Charles was referring to her unexpected appearance in Edmund's house on Monday night.

"Oh, no, what has she been up to now?" asked Miss Felicia, smiling at Annabelle who was trying to keep a calm expression on her face. Edmund had disappeared.

"Edmund's burglar alarm went off in the middle of the night on Monday. Naturally, I grabbed my shotgun and went down there to see what was going on."

"Naturally," said Miss Felicia, implying that Charles' reaction was somewhat overzealous.

He paused briefly as if surprised by her sarcasm.

"Go on," said Richter Davenport, Annabelle noting he was showing more interest in Charles' story than in any topic so far.

"Well, anyway, I went over there and who do I find fumbling around in the pitch black dark—Annabelle, here!"

Annabelle smiled sickly. "I needed to retrieve a valuable book I had loaned to Edmund. I was worried that it might get catalogued with the rest of his library."

"Annabelle, I can't believe you sometimes," said Felicia, shaking her head in dismay at Annabelle's notorious lack of common sense. "This crazy thing could have shot you," gesturing toward Charles who now looked rather sheepish. "Why on earth did you go over there in the middle of the night?"

"In the first place, it was not the *middle of the night*," said Annabelle, relieved that no one seemed to question the purpose of her visit, merely her timing. "It was around nine o'clock. I just forgot about the alarm system."

Miss Felicia scolded the young Master, "You ought to have called the police if you were concerned, Charles, and not gone running around in the dark with a firearm."

Annabelle smiled genuinely now. Miss Felicia, bless her, had taken the focus off of Annabelle's poor judgment and placed it squarely on Charles and his shotgun.

While Charles was sputtering in trying to defend himself to the older lady, Annabelle stole a glance at Richter Davenport. He did not seem amused in the slightest by Charles' discomfiture. In fact, he was staring directly at Annabelle. When she met his cold blue eyes, he gave her a slow, knowing smile. Annabelle took a gulp of her wine. Something about the man really gave her the creeps. "He looks as if he knows what I look like in my underwear, and he isn't impressed," she admitted to herself.

"Excuse me," she said to Felicia and Charles. "I need to find the 'hero' and speak to him for a moment." Annabelle moved away and into the crowded dining room, her desire to get some advice from Edmund about Nick outweighing her desire to escape Davenport.

Many people were already lined up in front of the buffet, drinks balanced carefully as they filled their plates with steaming food. Nick was not among them. Annabelle's stomach growled as she passed the diners, reminding her of the great deal of energy she had expended since her modest breakfast. She was tempted to stop and take a place in line, but decided she had better find Edmund and Nick first.

Annabelle walked into the foyer where she noticed a few hors d'oeuvres remaining on a silver tray. She grabbed three gratefully and stuffed them down, then moved on in search of

Nick. As she entered the living room and was scanning the group by the huge fireplace, she heard someone call her name.

"Annabelle! Hello, old girl!" It was Randall Dodge whom Annabelle suddenly realized she had not seen since the night of the Masters' Ball when she was looking for Edmund. She walked over and took his hand.

"I didn't realize you were out today," she said.

"I just got in last night", said Randall. Annabelle had heard that business commitments had kept Randall out of the county for the past several weeks. He had even missed Edmund's memorial service, but had sent a gigantic wreath as a token of remembrance.

"I hear you've been breaking and entering," said Randall with a grin. Annabelle was glad to see he was back to his usual manner of flirting and teasing with her instead of brushing her off as he had done on the night of the Masters' Ball.

"Oh, that," said Annabelle, inwardly furious with Charles for telling everyone about their little adventure at Edmund's. "Your crazy friend almost shot me!" she said, hoping to again change the focus from her odd behavior to Charles' spirited defense of Edmund's property.

The strategy didn't work so well this time.

"What were you doing there, Annabelle?" asked Randall, looking slyly at her.

She instinctively glanced away from him, knowing as she did so that she was betraying herself. She forced her eyes to meet his. "I was trying to locate an antique hunting book I had loaned Edmund. Didn't Charles tell you that part?"

"Yes, that's what he said, but I didn't quite buy it," said Randall. "I figured you were missing your 'sweetie' and went to look for his ghost."

Annabelle rolled her eyes, thinking how pleased and flattered Edmund would be by Randall's accusation. "No, I'm afraid I had a very practical reason for being there," said Annabelle, wishing to put an end to the discussion.

As it happened, Randall changed the subject himself. "Oh, Annabelle, I've been meaning to ask you something," he said, taking her elbow and easing a little closer as he spoke.

"Remember the night of the Ball when we met out in the gallery?"

Annabelle nodded. "Of course, I do. I haven't forgotten anything about that night."

Just at that moment, Nick joined them, scotch-and-soda in hand. He put his arm around Annabelle's waist. "My hero," he said, giving her a kiss.

"Nick! There you are! "I've been looking everywhere for you." Annabelle placed her hand on Randall's arm. "What were you going to ask me?"

It was as if a shade had been pulled down over Randall's eyes. "Nothing that won't wait", he replied, adding, "Nick, congratulations, old man!"

"Let's eat, darling," said Annabelle. "I'm famished!" Nick went with her obligingly. Although in her forties, Annabelle was as constantly hungry as when she was a teenager. At times, she shuddered to think what her weight would be if she ever stopped riding daily and working around their farm. After ten years of marriage, Nick appeared to accept her voracious appetite as a fact of life.

As the Farley's spooned fragrant stroganoff onto their plates, Annabelle heard Edmund's disembodied voice whisper in her ear.

"If he wants to know how you knew where the hounds would be, tell him you just went with the worst case scenario", he said. Annabelle nodded slightly, thankful that Edmund had hung-around and anticipated Nick's question.

It was not until they were comfortably seated beside one of the Robertson's hearths that she finally got to speak to her now famous husband. "Well, you're definitely the 'Hero of the Day', if not for the whole season," she said, smiling proudly at Nick.

He shook his head. "It was really not such a big deal. By the way, how did you know where those hounds were?"

Thanks to Edmund, Annabelle was ready with an answer. "I didn't really know where they were," she said modestly. "You have told me so many times that the worst thing that could happen to our hounds was for them to get loose on the interstate, so I thought we should go down there just in case. It was a lucky guess."

Nick looked closely at his wife. "It sure was a lucky guess. I suppose you've paid more attention to my talks about hounds than I realized."

"Of course I have, but really it was just dumb luck and I would hate for anyone to make a big thing out of it. I'm happy for you to take credit for this one."

This was a little unusual for Annabelle who generally a loved compliments and attention, especially from other foxhunters. But, on this occasion, her praise was sincere as she couldn't imagine herself playing Russian roulette with the interstate.

The Farley's lapsed into companionable silence and ate their meal by the crackling fire which Harold had made large enough to warm all of Guilford. Just as they were finishing their meal and, to Annabelle's horror, Randall Dodge and Charles Collins rushed over, obviously enthusiastic about something. Annabelle had no idea what she would say to Nick if her night time visit to Edmund's house was brought up yet again.   She looked around for guidance from her ghostly companion, but Edmund was across the room listening to a blonde undergrad from Vanderbilt University enthusiastically describing her first day of 'riding to hounds'. To Annabelle's intense relief, the two men had moved to another subject.

"Hey guys, some of us are going down to Waterford to hunt with Richter on Wednesday. Want to come with us?" Charles asked both Farley's.

"Some people in this Hunt still have to work for a living," said Nick, teasing the two younger men. In reality, he knew they both worked hard—Randall as an investment banker and Charles in a law practice—but it was fun to make them feel guilty anyway.

"Hey, I've hardly gotten to hunt at all this season. I've been so tied-up with work," said Randall, his face clouding briefly. "I've got some time off now and I want to go hunting," he said, brightening considerably as he made the announcement.

"Actually, I've got to be out of town this week," said Nick. "Annabelle may want to join you."

"Yes, go with us, Annabelle. We'll take care of her, Nick."

Annabelle shook her head. "I really don't think I want to go without Nick. I've gotten so spoiled with him driving the truck and trailer all of the time."

Richter Davenport strode into the room holding a full dinner plate and looked for a place to sit. Nick, always the gentleman, had finished his meal and offered his seat to the visiting Master.

"We're trying to persuade Annabelle to come to Waterford with us on Wednesday," said Charles with a grin, "but Nick has spoiled her so badly she can't remember how to pull a horse trailer". Annabelle looked at Richter who was now seated beside her, curious as to how he would react to the idea of her visiting his Hunt since it apparently hadn't been his idea.

"We'd love to have you hunt with us, Mrs. Farley," said Davenport suavely. He turned to Charles and Randall. "Can't one of you fellows pull a trailer for her?"

"Even better!" said Charles. "I'll ask Tiller to groom for us both, Annabelle. That way we can just have a good time and not worry about the horses."

Annabelle found that offer hard to resist. Despite his coolness, Annabelle was intrigued by Richter Davenport and thought he was perhaps warming up to her. Also, the offer of a groom meant that the hauling, saddling, and unsaddling of Samson would be done by someone else—in this case, a professional who had worked for Edmund and was now employed by Charles. He could probably care for Samson better than she could. Annabelle looked inquiringly at Nick.

"Oh, go on," said Nick, grinning at her. "You don't have to ask me."

"Are you sure you don't mind?" Annabelle liked to be asked, herself, so she prudently made it a practice to ask her husband's permission, especially when she felt sure it would be granted.

"I don't mind. You three just keep it to a dull roar," he said, including Randall and Charles in his lighthearted warning.

"This should be interesting, Kiddo," said a familiar voice in Annabelle's ear. This unexpected input from the spirit realm startled Annabelle who spilled red wine down the right leg of her beige hunting breeches.

"Gee, thanks!" she said angrily.

"What did *I* do?" asked Nick, looking bewildered at Charles and Randall.

"Oh, never mind," said Annabelle, getting up in annoyance to apply cold water to her breeches before they were permanently stained, leaving the fellows shaking their heads at her behavior.

"Women!" said Charles, and Edmund doubled over with glee.

CHAPTER IX
FIRESIDE CHAT

Sunday morning brought a steady downpour to the Guilford hunt country. The Farley's slept in, and when they finally roused around ten o'clock, Nick cooked a breakfast of scrambled eggs, bacon, and his special homemade biscuits. He had intended to retreat to the quiet of his study to work on a brief he needed to finish, but Annabelle had begged a favor of him to build a fire for her in the tack room at the stable. Since Nick had work to do, she had decided to spend the rainy Sunday cleaning saddles and bridles.

The Farley's stable was Annabelle's favorite place on the 50 acre farm. It had six horse stalls, a full bath, and a tack room with a working fireplace. Annabelle had decorated the tack room's office with old hunting prints, mounted fox masks, and other hunting memorabilia. Wooden saddle and bridle racks handcrafted by a local carpenter completed the practical, well-designed effect.

She had never been keen on cleaning anything, especially muddy saddles, but that had changed now that she could work in her favorite room by a crackling fire. Friends had initially been surprised at Nick's indulgence, as having a fireplace in a barn could be dangerous for the unwary, but Annabelle had promised to be careful and there was certainly an improvement in the Farley's turn-out.

Today, as Annabelle settled down to work on Samson's over-sized hunting bridle, she began to go over the events of the previous day in her mind. She was proud of Nick's success in saving the hounds, and also proud of how well she, with Edmund's advice, had handled such a dangerous experience.

She did not think of herself as a bold rider. She had taken up the sport late in life, unlike the majority of foxhunters who had started riding as tots and had been members of Pony Clubs throughout their childhood. Several Hill County members had even raced or ridden stadium jumpers as professionals. Annabelle knew she could never compete with the experience and talent of the best of them, but she loved to jump the small jumps in her riding arena and hoped that one day she would find the courage to ride Samson in First Flight. He had performed so brilliantly during the excitement of rescuing the hounds that she felt more and more it was only a matter of overcoming her own timidity.

Annabelle also felt proud of her own performance during other adventures of the past week. Although she had been shocked when Charles pointed a gun in her face, she hadn't panicked, but had kept her wits about her and removed the fax that Edmund needed. In fact, she had actually grabbed all four of the papers that had ejected from the machine, one of which Edmund had confirmed as being sent by the murderer. She had then placed them within the pages of the antique book she had swiped from Edmund's library and hid the book safely in her underwear drawer. She had gotten the idea of keeping all of the evidence exactly in the same order in which it was removed from the house by watching Court TV. She pictured herself as the glamorous star witness testifying in court, wearing something chic and black and slenderizing in case the trial was televised.

She continued to work while fantasizing and unfastened all of the buckles and removed the bit from the bridle. She left the bit to soak in a bowl of warm, soapy water and attacked the mud-caked leather with glycerin soap and a barely dampened sponge. As labor intensive as the technique was, Annabelle knew that the least amount of water used on the leather, the longer it would last. As she began on the reins, still musing about her outfit for the trial, she suddenly felt she was not alone.

Sure enough, Edmund had joined her and was seated on an old wooden chair in his red coat, looking for all the world like a lank figure come to life from one of her antique hunting prints.

"What a day we had yesterday!" he said heartily, without wasting time on a more traditional greeting. "You did a good job of listening to me, Kiddo, and we saved those hounds, together! Now—let's get busy capturing my murderer. We have the fax and I had thought you could just take it to the police, but now I want to see what Randall Dodge gets up to on Wednesday."

Annabelle frowned as she cleaned the bit. She assumed Edmund was referring to her invitation to accompany Randall and Charles to hunt with the Waterford. "So you think he invited me to hunt with him for some nefarious reason, not just because he enjoys my company?"

"He no doubt enjoys your company, my dear", said Edmund, "but the last time he saw you he had just returned from pushing me down the stairs. You told me he acted pre-occupied and was downright unfriendly. Don't think for a moment he has forgotten that little meeting."

Annabelle remembered Randall's comment from the night before and had to admit he was probably right. "I still don't see why he would ask me to hunt," she said stubbornly. "What is the Waterford country like, anyway?"

"It's a little like Guilford, but not quite as hilly. Actually, there isn't much country left. Davenport is in a hell of a situation."

Annabelle raised her head from putting the pieces of the bridle together and looked at Edmund. "What do you mean? By the way, that man makes me really uncomfortable."

"Waterford Hounds is about out of territory to hunt. They lost their last big tract of land just after the first of this year." Edmund shook his head. "It's a great shame. They're one of the oldest packs in the country."

"But he hasn't been Master there all that long, has he? It seems I heard that he was a Master of a Virginia Hunt at one time . . ."

"No, he's only been there a few years. He's not an easy chap to get along with, but I've known him most of his life. In fact, I believe I'm the one who convinced him he could hunt hounds . . ."

"I'm sure that's true," said Annabelle, wanting to keep Edmund on topic. "But didn't I hear that Waterford had plenty of hunt country until he became Master, then the landowners started selling off one by one?"

"Yes, I've heard that. And as facts go, it's true. But there could be any number of reasons people might sell their land. It's convenient to blame whoever's in charge of the Hunt at the time, but landowner relationships take decades to develop."

Edmund got a sly look on his face. "Why the sudden interest in Davenport? I'm not so sure I believe he makes you feel uncomfortable. I saw you giving him the once-over yesterday."

Annabelle was flattered by his apparent jealousy and tried to suppress a grin. "I think he's the one who's interested in me," she said, feigning innocence. "He was certainly curious about my being caught in your house the other night."

"Well, of course he was!" Edmund laughed. "You have to admit that's a funny story." He slapped his knee in amusement.

Annabelle looked at him. "If you ever, *ever* get me in a situation like that again, I'll . . ."

"You'll kill me?" Edmund laughed even more at his own humor, which was always his favorite.

"That husband of yours is quite a 'hound man'!" he said, changing the subject when he saw his joke hadn't entertained her. "I knew when I nominated him to be a Joint Master he had great deeds in him! Now, no one can deny it!"

Annabelle finished Samson's bridle and began on King's. She was glad Edmund had brought up the subject of Nick's Mastership.

"Did someone doubt it at the time?" she asked. Annabelle had dearly wanted Nick to be asked to be a Master—so much so that she had deliberately distanced herself from the situation for fear of somehow spoiling his chances. At the same time she had wondered if Edmund had promoted the idea because of his interest in her and had often thought of asking him outright.

"Not so much, but you know foxhunters—wary of anything, or anyone, new."

Annabelle knew what he meant, but had never really understood it. "Why do you suppose that is, Edmund?" she asked, all the while continuing to work.

"Well, there are lots of reasons. For one thing, foxhunting is a sport based on tradition and rules that haven't changed for hundreds of years. People who are interested in a sport like that aren't impressed with the new or the modern like most other people are, or they'd be doing something else."

"Like rollerblading?" asked Annabelle wryly.

"Exactly," said Edmund. "Then, I think there's always the concern that new people won't love the sport like the old-timers do, and won't fight to preserve it or might even want to change it in some way. And, change usually doesn't bode well for the sport of foxhunting."

"How do you mean?"

"Well, most of the changes in recent years have been in the form of land development that has practically devoured all of the country suitable for foxhunting. Some hunts have gone completely out of existence because their territory was sold out from under them, bit by bit. Look at the Waterford Hounds, for instance. Speaking of the Waterford", he said as if just remembering the task at hand, "what's the plan for this Wednesday? You should have some excellent opportunities to further our objective." This was Edmund's tactful term for solving his own murder.

"I don't have a plan, yet," said Annabelle, laying King's freshly cleaned bridle aside and turning to face Edmund. "And, I don't mind telling you I'm a little bit nervous about this whole thing. Now that—thanks to Charles—everyone knows I was snooping around Huntersleigh last week, Randall may realize I know what's up."

"Oh, no, Annabelle," said Edmund. "I don't think he would suspect you, of all people. He probably just wants to make friendly so you won't tattle on him about being out in the hallway the night of my murder. Besides, how could you have known what to look for at my house if I hadn't told you—and I'm supposed to be dead, remember?"

"You are dead, otherwise you wouldn't be in my tack room wearing a white tie and scarlet. Seriously, Edmund, people knew we were friends. He may think you told me all about your business dealings."

Edmund's eyes twinkled. "You mean people knew you had a crush on me! No one who knew me would believe I would waste my time talking with you about business!" He gave her a ghostly wink and began to disappear.

"Wait! I want to ask you something, you old sexist", but then realized she was alone. She sighed in exasperation and began working on Samson's muddy saddle.

CHAPTER X

A DAY WITH THE WATERFORD HOUNDS

"You cain't always get what you *wa-a-nt*," sang Randall. "You cain't always get what you *wa-a-nt*, but if you try sometimes . . ."

"Please!" Annabelle said. "Mick Jagger is rolling over in his grave and he's not even dead yet!"

"He's probably rolling over next to some supermodel," Charles said wistfully.

The three foxhunters were heading to hunt with the Waterford Hounds in Charles' SUV with Charles at the wheel, Annabelle in the passenger seat, and Randall hanging between them from the back seat like an impatient five year old, providing entertainment in the form of horrendous vocal accompaniment to the Rolling Stones.

Tiller had picked up Samson earlier that morning and would have him tacked up for the hunt at 1:00, so Annabelle had nothing to do but enjoy herself and to keep her eyes and ears open for clues. Perhaps Randall would do or say something incriminating she could later relay to the police, but the talk had been lighthearted chatter with some tales of Edmund thrown in, nothing Annabelle hadn't heard before on at least one other occasion. Never the most patient of souls, Annabelle decided to do a little 'fishing'.

"So, Randall, are you still making millions for people?" she asked playfully.

"Oh, yes," Randall replied with a complacent little smile. "I've picked up a new client in the past few days and I've already put him onto something really hot."

"Oh, that's good," said Annabelle, dying to ask the identity of the lucky individual, but knowing he wouldn't tell.

"Anything I might be interested in?" she asked, trying a slightly different tactic.

"Oh, I don't know. Doesn't Nick handle your investments for you? Besides, this deal is highly speculative."

"Well, you know me. I love a little risk."

"No you don't!" Randall and Charles said in unison, then burst-out laughing.

"You're the most cautious foxhunter I know," said Charles, patting Annabelle on the arm so she would understand that he loved her anyway.

The conversation turned to a discussion of Annabelle's various quirks and foibles and away from investment banking and Randall's new client. The miles sped away as Charles headed for what was left of Waterford's hunting country—once many thousands of acres but now reduced so considerably that the Meet today was to be held on the last remaining tract of any size. Annabelle looked out of the window at the passing subdivisions and their signs advertising the perfect home with community clubhouse and pool, all for less than two hundred thousand dollars. She shuddered to think a similar fate could be waiting for Guilford if the members weren't diligent about protecting precious open spaces.

Charles turned in between two housing developments and finally the dwellings began to slightly thin out slightly. He pulled up to the kennel grounds and found there was hardly a place to park in the cramped area.

"I'm glad Tiller brought the horses and I don't have to get a trailer in here," said Charles, glancing around at the crowded conditions. "I'm having a hard enough time finding a spot for this thing."

"There's Miss Felicia!" said Annabelle, gladly. "I didn't know she was hunting here today."

"Actually, I invited her last night," said Randall. "I thought Charles' great big trailer could hold another horse."

"Oh, it was no problem," said Charles. "It made more work for Tiller, but he was gracious about it."

"I need to give him a generous tip", thought Annabelle. Four horses to haul and tack up was quite a bit of work.

"Why didn't Felicia come with us?" asked Annabelle, who would have enjoyed the hour or so in her friend's company.

"Oh, you know her—she said she wanted her own vehicle in case we decided to stay all evening."

"Is there a party after the hunt?"

"I don't think so—at least not like ours. I think a few folks just stand around with a beer and talk."

"Oh, well," said Annabelle, disappointed. "Yet another reason to prefer hunting with Hill County", she thought to herself.

Charles finally found a spot and they disembarked. Miss Felicia strode up, looking jaunty and fit in her old-fashioned tan breeches that were flared at the hips like Cavalry twills. The dress for weekday hunts is usually informal and allows a little more self expression than the regimented attire required for formal Meets. Felicia took full advantage of this leeway by wearing a tattersall vest, a multi-colored stock tie, and tweed coat. Every garment had been tailored for her in London and was at least twenty years old. The effect was charming in a British country house sort of way.

"Thought you kids would never get here," she said in her booming voice that had tally-hoed many a fox over the years.

"We've been looking for a place to park for twenty minutes," said Charles, exaggerating only a little.

"I know." Felicia shook her head. "I feel really sorry for these folks. Oh, well, let's quit complaining and get on with the hunt."

Tiller had the four horses saddled, bridled, and tied alongside Charles' long aluminum trailer. Annabelle appreciated having her horse made ready for her, but she wished they had arrived in time for her to mount up and ride Samson for a few minutes before moving off. She hated being rushed before a hunt as it always made her feel she was forgetting something important. This was especially true in a strange place without her trailer's well-organized tack compartment. Annabelle got a twenty-dollar bill out of her purse for Tiller, and as she did she remembered the important 'something' she had indeed forgotten—her flask!

"Oh, no!" she wailed.

Charles looked around, concern on his face. "What's wrong?"

"I forgot my flask!" said Annabelle in anguish. Drinking from a flask is an old hunting tradition with the dual purpose of keeping the hunters warm in cold weather, and fortifying their courage while participating in a dangerous sport. There are even specific types of leather flask-holders that attach to hunting saddles that are different for women than for men. Many old hunting books contain recipes for mixtures to fill them with, the most well known called Hound's Blood, a combination of brandy and ruby port. The amount any foxhunter indulged in this particular tradition varied, but everyone knew that Annabelle was a tippler who rarely started a hunt without a full flask, regardless of the weather or riding conditions.

"Oh, for heaven's sake", said Charles, who carried the correct men's flask on his saddle more for looks than use as he certainly did not need 'liquid courage'. "You can share with the rest of us. Besides, the way these folks move on, you won't have time to drink, anyway."

"Oh, no," said Annabelle again, thinking from the sound of things that she would need her flask even more than usual. It was her theory that the more relaxed she was, the better she rode. "Nothing to do about it now," she thought to herself. She saw Tiller holding Samson next to the mounting block for her to get on, and would do the same for Miss Felicia, Charles, and Randall.

"Thank you so much for helping me today, Tiller," said Annabelle as she slipped him a folded bill.

"Thank *you*, Miss Annabelle," he replied, tipping his trademark cowboy hat.

Annabelle moved Samson away from the block. He was excited today, sensing they were in new territory and among the smells of unfamiliar Waterford horses. She walked him around, knowing that forcing him to stand still would make him agitated. There was not really enough time for him to settle down before Annabelle heard the Master call everyone to gather for the Meet.

She looked through the crowd for the familiar sight of Miss Felicia on her ancient thoroughbred and rode up to her side. She intended to stick there like glue, at least until Samson relaxed.

The Master of the Waterford Hounds said very little by way of introduction, merely stating he had twelve and a half couple of hounds out that day and that they would begin drawing the covert to the west. Annabelle smiled at the foxhunting lingo that referred to hounds in pairs—twelve and a half couple indicated twenty-five hounds. As Annabelle sat her restive horse, Davenport asked Charles, as a visiting Master, to ride at his side. He tipped his cap to the other Hill County guests and took off at a brisk trot toward the woods. Randall followed close behind in First Flight with Annabelle and Felicia staying back in Second.

Unlike Warren Fitzpatrick, Waterford's Second Flight Field Master pulled in directly behind the last of the First Flight riders who soon moved their pace from a brisk trot to a gallop. Annabelle realized what Charles had meant when he said she wouldn't have time for her flask, and the hounds weren't even chasing anything yet!

She wondered if they would run anything. It was not unusual for February in the south to have a few warm days, a precursor to the coming springtime. Although it was a beautiful sunny afternoon, the conditions were not ideal for running a coyote.

Annabelle felt unsure of herself so held Samson on a tight rein. The terrain was not as steep as Hill County's, but it was trappy to negotiate, nonetheless. It seemed that every few hundred yards there was a deep, rocky streambed to cross, and, unlike Hill County's well maintained trails, the paths through the woods could hardly be called paths at all, being more like obstacle courses of fallen trees and broken limbs that barred the way strategically at head level for most riders.

After about fifteen minutes, Annabelle's tweed coat was splashed with mud, she had a bleeding scratch on her cheek from failing to duck in a timely manner, and she was thoroughly enjoying herself.

"It appears you didn't need a drink after all," said a warm voice in Annabelle's ear. "You're doing very well without it!"

"Why thank you Edmund," she said, doubting she would be overheard in the commotion of galloping hooves.

Then, to her surprise, Edmund was seated comfortably behind her on Samson's generous back, and she thought she could feel his arms wrapped around her waist.

"We should have tried this when I was alive, Kiddo," and she imagined she felt him give her a little squeeze.

They finally stopped for a moment in a small clearing, the horses sweating heavily in the warm sunshine. Most foxhunters clip their horses' winter coats in anticipation of such spring-like days. When a horse's heavy winter coat becomes wet with perspiration, it is itchy and uncomfortable if the weather is warm. Annabelle was glad she had recently clipped Samson, knowing his closely cropped coat would soon dry in the sun.

Randall trotted back from First Flight and joined the ladies. "Annabelle, would you like a 'wee nip of the creature'?" Randall asked, and began removing his flask from its leather case.

"I certainly would!" said Annabelle, whose throat was dry from excitement and exertion.

Unfortunately, the Field Master chose that moment to take off.

"That man doesn't believe in easing off slowly does he?" asked Miss Felicia, galloping alongside Annabelle and Randall.

"One of these days I'll tell you a little story about her," said Edmund. "I knew her pretty well when I was alive." Annabelle thought it best to ignore him with her friends in such close proximity.

"No," she answered Miss Felicia, and wanting to let Edmund know she was glad of his presence she added, "and though it seems a little pointless since we aren't even on a run, I *am* having a wonderful time!"

"Annabelle, I need to ask you something," said Randall, riding close to her knee.

"Okay", she replied, thinking his timing was poor but curious to hear what he had to say.

"I just need to know if you told anyone about what happened at the Ball?"

Annabelle started to answer, but they had reached a streambed that was bordered on each bank by a muddy slope. Annabelle had no choice but to follow Miss Felicia, who was already halfway across. At the moment, all of her attention was required to negotiate the crossing, even Samson needing guidance.

No sooner were they on top of the opposite bank than they heard a hound cry out. Within moments another hound seconded, followed by what sounded like the entire pack.

Miss Felicia looked back over her shoulder at Annabelle. "You'd better keep your eyes up, your heels down, and your seat well in the saddle," she said with a grin.

Before Annabelle could guess what she meant, she saw Felicia's horse jump up and over a huge log lying directly across the path. Samson was right on her horse's tail with no time for Annabelle to chicken-out and try to pull him up. She instinctively grabbed a handful of her horse's generous draft horse mane, and in a split-second they were over the log and galloping away on the other side. Apparently, ghosts didn't weigh all that much. Annabelle was so delighted that she broke a cardinal rule in the hunting field and yelled like an Indian. Fortunately, the Field was moving too fast for many to hear except Felicia, who told her to 'pipe down and ride'.

"Don't worry, dear," said Edmund. "She's just jealous because you're keeping up with her!"

CHAPTER XI
AN UNFORTUNATE END TO A PERFECT DAY

Annabelle felt her day was made. She had finally taken Samson over a jump in the hunt field! Although it was a log, and it wasn't the same as jumping a coop, it was certainly a start. As they continued to fly after the hounds she grinned from ear to ear, putting herself in danger of a mud-ball in her teeth, but not caring in the slightest. Edmund appeared to be having as much fun as Annabelle—at least it sounded that way from the encouragement he was shouting into her ear as they galloped along.

The run was not to last, however. The heat and poor scenting conditions took their toll, so after about twenty minutes the hounds lost their quarry and were silent again. Annabelle was glad for a rest and sat musing happily with Edmund over her log-jumping success when Randall trotted up.

"I heard you yelling," he said, pulling out his flask. "Was that fear or triumph?"

"Pure triumph," she said proudly. She took the flask and drank a long draught.

"Not too much, Kiddo", Edmund said in her ear. "You've done perfectly well without it today."

"This is a celebration!" said Annabelle, addressing herself both to Edmund and her living friends.

Felicia joined them, her own flask in hand. "I would like to propose a toast," she said in formal tones. "We've found out today that chickens really can fly!"

They all laughed, even Annabelle.

"I don't care how much you tease me, we *did* it!" She patted Samson's big brown neck before taking a sip from Miss Felicia's flask. She knew what a compliment it was. Felicia rarely shared her flask with others, nor did she partake when offered. Her fastidiousness was well known.

The Field Master moved off almost before she could return the precious object. "You can't keep it, Annabelle," said Felicia jokingly as Annabelle returned the small sterling silver rectangle.

Annabelle feigned dismay. "Darn!"

Felicia dexterously replaced the flask into the leather case on her saddle and away they cantered.

As they rode off after the frenetic Field Master, Annabelle wished they would slow down long enough for her to chat with Randall. Just as Edmund had predicted, he was very concerned about what she had seen on the night of the Masters' Ball. She smiled grimly, looking forward to what he had to say. She pushed back her helmet and wiped her forehead on her coat sleeve, suddenly feeling very hot with sweat breaking out on her face. She wished she could take her helmet off as it made her head feel so heavy, and she wished she could halt.

"Felicia!" she yelled as loud as she could, the effort making her feel even more ill. Unfortunately, their pace was such that she did not hear.

"Miss *Felicia!*" she cried again, almost choking this time.

The woman looked over her shoulder at Annabelle and pulled back on her reins, stopping her horse in his tracks.

"Annabelle, you're white as a sheet!", and turned-back to ride alongside her ailing friend.

"What's wrong?", asked Randall, holding a tight rein on his prancing horse who was ready to get going with the rest of the Field.

"I'm sick," said Annabelle weakly, falling forward on her horse's neck.

"What on earth? Here, you'd better get down."

Felicia dismounted in a flash and grabbed Samson's reins. "Go on, Randall", she said. "She's just overheated. She'll be all right in a minute. I'll wait with her until she's feeling better."

"You're sure?" Randall replied, fighting his horse as it danced and pulled.

"I'm sure. Go on."

"Okay," and, to his horse's relief, they left in a gallop.

Personally, Annabelle wasn't so sure she would be all right in a matter of minutes. She struggled to dismount from and then stood, leaning against her horse's side. Through waves of nausea she noticed Edmund had also dismounted (actually he had just disappeared from Samson's back and then reappeared to stand beside her). He looked thoroughly bewildered and a little disappointed, like a child whose favorite game had been interrupted for no apparent reason.

"What's wrong, Annabelle?" he asked. "I thought we were doing so well…"

"Come, sit down and move away from that hot horse," said Miss Felicia. She loosened the chinstrap on Annabelle's helmet and eased her onto a fallen log. Annabelle had let herself be led like a child and sat obediently where Felicia indicated, too nauseated to even attempt to answer Edmund.

"Here, have a swig of this," said Felicia, handing her the sterling flask. Annabelle drank some, but wished for something cold. She took a deep breath and put her head in her hands, then began to loosen her stock tie.

Felicia sat down beside her, holding both horses' reins in one hand and patting Annabelle's shoulder with the other. Suddenly, Annabelle knew she was going to vomit.

"Edmund, I'm going to be sick," she gasped, while jumping to her feet and turning away from the older woman. She vomited violently into the leaves behind where they'd been sitting.

"Honey, we need to get you back to the trailers," said Felicia. "I think you're hallucinating. Can you walk?"

"Just let me sit here for a minute, Miss Felicia," said Annabelle weakly. She sat back down on the log and leaned forward, head in hands again. She could feel her face slick with sweat. The older woman continued to hold the horses while making soothing noises to Annabelle. Edmund was gazing at her in distress. After a short time, Annabelle took a deep breath and stood up.

"I feel a little better," she said cautiously.

"Well, don't rush it," said Felicia. "Do you think you can walk back to the trailer?"

"How far is it?"

"It's probably a little over a mile."

Annabelle took another deep breath. As sick as she was, she was awed at the amazing sense of direction possessed by many lifelong foxhunters. She looked doubtfully down at her field boots. They were one of her prized possessions—custom cordovan leather with Spanish tops and were incredibly comfortable to ride in. They were not, however, made for walking long distances. She looked at Samson who was calmly munching greenery within his reach.

"I think I'd like to try and ride," said Annabelle.

"You're sure? I don't mind walking," said Felicia. "I can lead both horses."

"No, I want to try and ride. It will be so much faster and probably easier than trying to walk in these boots—if my stomach can take it."

"Well, that's certainly true. You want to try and mount?"

"Yes. Just hold him for me."

Miss Felicia chuckled. "I'll hold this wild thing. He seems about to bolt any minute."

Annabelle smiled and put her foot in the stirrup. She hesitated just a moment and then pulled herself up into the saddle. She sat quietly for a second, took a few deep breaths, and then took the reins from Felicia.

"I think I'll be okay to ride if we just walk. It'll still be quicker than going on foot."

"Fine with me," said the older woman, climbing on her horse.

The two rode in silence, negotiating the streams and logs they had galloped across earlier at a very careful pace this time. Annabelle felt weak and light-headed, grateful for Samson's steady, plodding gait. He seemed to sense the need to go even more carefully than usual.

"That young lad is worth his weight in gold," said a familiar voice in her ear, "and that would be a considerable amount of gold."

Annabelle managed a smile. "I was wondering if you were around," she said softly.

"What? You okay, dear?" asked Felicia over her shoulder.

"I just asked how much further."

"Not much. Look—you can see the trailers through those trees."

"Oh, thank goodness."

In a few minutes, they were there. Annabelle slid from the saddle and handed the reins to Tiller who had been sitting inside Charles' truck fiddling with the radio when they rode up. Surprised, he had jumped out of the cab and met them.

"What happened, ladies? Did one of your horses throw a shoe?"

"No, Tiller," answered Miss Felicia. "Annabelle got to feeling bad so I brought her in. She's just overheated."

"I'm sorry, Miss Annabelle", said Tiller, as he tied Samson to the trailer. "Would you like a cold drink?"

"Oh, do you have one? That would be great. Thanks, Tiller." Annabelle gratefully accepted the cold Coke.

"Tiller, we'll leave the horses with you. I'm going to take Annabelle on home. Tell the boys for us, will you?" Miss Felicia unlocked her twenty year old pickup truck and climbed in.

"Yes, Ma'am," said Tiller, and began unsaddling Winston, Felicia's horse.

"Oh, Tiller," said Miss Felicia. "Put my tack in the back of the truck, will you? I'll get started on cleaning it when I get home."

Annabelle shook her head in amazement at Felicia's dedication, and thought she would certainly not be doing any tack cleaning of her own, today.

"Ready, Annabelle?" Felicia prepared to start the old Ford.

"Ready as I'll ever be," answered Annabelle, climbing into the passenger seat, still feeling queasy and listless. She dreaded the long ride home when   normally she would have loved spending an hour alone with Miss Felicia.

"Thank you so much for helping me," she said to her friend. "I'm sorry I caused you to miss so much of the hunt. I'll try to make it up to you in some way."

"Nonsense," said Felicia firmly. "They've already had the best run they'll have all day and we were there for it. It's too hot to hunt, anyway."

Annabelle, feeling deeply appreciative but still uncomfortable, settled down with her drink for the long ride home. Edmund had been invisible after she threw-up, and he seemed to have disappeared altogether. "Just like a man," she thought, as if he would have been any help to her.

CHAPTER XII
MOTIVE AND OPPORTUNITY

Annabelle woke the next morning still feeling weak, but hungry. She'd gone to bed early after having a supper of Pepto-Bismol and another Coke, and downplayed her sick spell to Nick when he'd called. Surprisingly, she'd slept well and felt ready for a big breakfast, but, out of caution, she decided to have only a toasted bagel even though she craved a large plate of bacon and eggs.

As she sat down to her meal, Edmund appeared on the window seat with his arms crossed, watching her.

"Good morning," said Annabelle, biting into the bagel.

"Good morning yourself!   I thought for a while yesterday you were going to join me on the other side."

Annabelle paused, bagel in hand. "What do you mean? When I jumped that log?"

"No, no.   Don't you realize he tried to kill you yesterday?"

The bagel fell back onto the breakfast plate.

Her mouth dropped open and her eyes widened—"D-d-do you really think so?"

"I certainly do. Randall attempted to poison you with port from his flask. The fact that you threw-up so quickly is what kept you from getting any sicker."

"Oh, Edmund, I don't know. In the first place, why would he want to kill *me?*" Annabelle shook her head, which immediately began to ache. "Well, you are right about one thing. I didn't just get overheated, as Miss Felicia kept

100

insisting, and I noticed you didn't hang around too long after I was sick."

"Annabelle, you know I can't stand the sight of vomit. As for Felicia Blackwell, I've known her all of my life and, as 'dear as she is', she's never been long on imagination." Edmund leaned back against the window and smiled with a faraway look in his eyes. "Did you know I asked her to marry me once? She had just won her first point-to-point race and I was overcome with admiration."

Annabelle smirked. "What number would she have been on the list? Ten?"

Edmund smirked back, "One, actually. I was only sixteen at the time. You know she's quite a few years older than I am—*was*," he corrected himself. "Felicia was the daughter of one of the founding members of this Hunt, an heiress who chased foxes since the 1940's."

"Edmund, I would love to hear all about your childhood romance, but you've just told me you think someone tried to kill me yesterday. I'd appreciate it if you would expound on that statement just a little before you get caught up on a trek down memory lane.

"You're right, of course," said Edmund, genially. "Well, we know Charles told Randall you had been snooping around Huntersleigh because he asked you about it at the Robertson's after the hunt on Saturday, right?"

"Yes," Annabelle agreed. "But he thought I was there because I was missing you. At least that's what he said."

"That's what he said, but I'll bet he's remembered sending me that fax by now and had been hoping to retrieve it, himself. He probably assumes I talked to you about my business dealings."

"Hmmph," Annabelle cleared her throat loudly. "It seems to me I said that very thing on Sunday when we were talking in the tack room and you pooh-poohed the idea."

"That was before he tried to poison you."

"You mean I was right? Is that what you're trying to tell me?"

"Now that we have more evidence, it appears that you did guess correctly," said Edmund airily. "Anyway, let me continue."

Annabelle snorted derisively, but let him go on.

"He's also been very concerned about the fact that you encountered him entering the Ballroom just minutes before you found me at the foot of the Pierre's staircase."

"That's certainly true," said Annabelle. "He's been trying to quiz me about whether or not I shared that little detail with anyone."

"*Anyone like the 'NYPD'* is what he really wants to know. He was the last person to see me alive, but he omitted that fact when he was questioned—claimed to be in the men's room."

"Wouldn't he feel pretty safe after the coroner ruled your death an accident?" asked Annabelle.

"You're thinking like an innocent person, my dear. You must remember that this man has a guilty conscience. He's not thinking rationally."

"I know, I know. I've read my share of mystery novels. The murderer appears to be totally in the clear, but then he cracks and tells on himself. I've always thought it was a little silly, frankly. I think if I killed someone and had gotten away with it, I'd just thank my lucky stars and move on to other things."

"Spoken with the true innocence of a clear conscience!" Edmund replied. "What's the worst thing you've ever done to anyone, Annabelle, edged them out of first place in a best dressed contest?"

"I resent that. You have a fairly low opinion of my interests." She thought for a moment. "I guess you're right, though. I feel guilty if I think I've hurt someone's feelings at a dinner party."

"You definitely wouldn't make a successful killer, Kiddo, and this man won't either. He's much too emotional. He was feeling guilty about MotionTech when he confessed his concerns to me at dinner that night, or none of this would have happened."

Annabelle nodded in agreement. On the night Edmund had first appeared in her kitchen, he'd told her he had been pushed down the stairs at the Pierre Hotel by Randall Dodge, the suave New Yorker and Edmund's friend. Edmund had been about to reveal the truth to the other Hill County members about a certain investment deal Randall had put together. He and Randall had clashed at dinner one night at Edmund's house right before the Ball when Edmund had refused to keep his concerns a secret.

Randall had persuaded several of Hill County's wealthiest members, including Edmund, to invest large sums of money in a small, closely-held corporation called MotionTech that claimed to have rights to a new technology, something related to motion-generating properties in the molecular structure of certain substances, particularly those used in making explosives. Randall had assured his clients there was a huge market for such technology in detecting possible threats to homeland security after the terror attacks on September 11th. While this was true as far as it went, he failed to mention MotionTech had no Federal patent for that particular technology and, more importantly, there was no actual product to sell. What they had was a good idea, and that was all.

Reminding Annabelle again of the events that led up to Randall sending him the incriminating fax, Edmund said, "One night last January, Randall came down from New York to hunt and he and I had partaken generously of my best wine. Really soused, he told me that not only MotionTech did not have a patent, but that he had recently learned the prospect of being granted one was looking pretty doubtful."

Annabelle listened carefully as Edmund continued. "Upon sobering up the next day, Randall attempted to swear me to secrecy, but I declined. I felt Randall owed it to the other investors, some of whom were my lifelong hunting friends, to tell them the truth about MotionTech's prospects. Randall returned to New York, furiously claiming I felt more loyal to my old friends than to him, but before the week was out he called me full of apologies. He even asked for my help."

Annabelle was aware that Edmund did not hold grudges. His tolerant attitude towards others had earned him forgiveness for his own transgressions on too many occasions. This time was no different. Edmund had agreed to intercede with the other investors in Randall's behalf on one condition—he wanted the complete financial breakdown regarding MotionTech as to who had invested and in what amounts, the financial balance sheet of the company, and exactly what the prospects were for success. Randall had gratefully agreed to fax him the information that day, and had been as good as his word.

However, the numbers on the fax showed a company deeply in debt and a group of investors who stood to lose their entire capital investments, some of which were quite large. Over half of the capital had been raised through Randall's Hill County connections. There was also a personal apology from Randall Dodge handwritten at the bottom of the page.

Annabelle and Edmund recollected the ensuing tragedy. The following week, Edmund and Randall had both attended the Masters Ball in New York. As everyone else was laughing and chatting upon entering the Ballroom, Randall had held Edmund back and at first expressed his appreciation to Edmund for agreeing to help him. He then attempted to persuade Edmund to keep his secret, arguing that the entire corporation would collapse if the Hill County investors withdrew their funding. Edmund was even less inclined to keep his friends in the dark after seeing the financial sheet and they had argued bitterly, making Edmund late for his dinner speech and eventually leading to his fatal shove down the staircase.

Annabelle was not particularly interested in new technology unless it related to cookware or hair dryers, and her only experience with homeland security involved being insulted about the size of her makeup case. She did understand that no patent and no product meant no return on an investment, and why her friend, Randall Dodge, the man she felt was the height of New York sophistication, might feel threatened enough by her knowledge of his crimes to try to kill her. It was a sobering thought, to say the least, although she reflected if choosing a costume for eternity, her tweed coat and field boots would have done nicely as they would have been a perfect complement to Edmund's scarlet and white ensemble.

"So you think he fed me poison out of his flask?"

"I do."

"Do you think it's time for me to tell Nick about all of this?" she asked. "Maybe he could help us. I don't seem to be doing too well on my own."

Edmund was silent for a moment. "Yes, I've always had a great deal of confidence in Nick Farley. He'll be furious with Randall for trying to hurt you, but he's not one to lose his head and do anything rash. Yes, I think you should tell him as soon as he gets home."

Annabelle sighed with relief. She, too, felt confident in Nick's abilities, especially when it came to protecting her.

"Well, I'm glad that's settled, then. And, boy, am I glad I threw up yesterday!"

"Me, too, Kiddo, me, too!" With that, Edmund gave a pat in the general direction of Annabelle's head and faded slowly out of sight, leaving the comfortable padded window seat to the two terriers. Except for Annabelle, they, alone, seemed to know it had been previously occupied.

Annabelle decided to have a second bagel. She deserved it—she was almost killed yesterday! She sat musing and munching, resolving to live every day to its fullest as she had heard many people say when they've had a brush with their own mortality. However, instead of frightening her and making her more cautious, the experience left her strangely energized. She resolved to bring Edmund's killer to justice, and she was more determined than ever to ride Samson in First Flight before the season was over—she was tired of being afraid and hanging back. Who knew how many chances she would have to do the things that needed to be done?

She also was, despite her cool attitude in front of Edmund, very hurt to think that Randall Dodge would plot to kill her in cold blood. Putting poison in a flask was not the spontaneous act of an angry person—it took planning and preparation—yet she had known for weeks he had pushed Edmund down the stairs at the Pierre. Many conflicting emotions were rolling around in her head, so she decided some activity would help clear it.

One thing she didn't particularly want to do, though unfortunately necessary, was to clean her mud-splattered tack. The streams and gullies at Waterford had gotten it filthy.

She finished her second bagel and was putting on her Barbour coat to go to the barn when the telephone rang. She answered it happily, glad for an excuse to put off the inevitable.

"Hello, Annabelle?" It was Shelley Fitzpatrick.

"Hey there, what have you been up to?"

"Listen, Annabelle, I have some very bad news. Warren thought you should be among the first to know."

Annabelle sat back down at the table. She couldn't imagine what Shelley would say next.

"Go ahead," she said, grimly, feeling that nothing much could faze her after Edmund's murder and her own brush with death only the day before.

"Miss Felicia is dead. Her housekeeper found her this morning."

CHAPTER XIII
BLACKWOOD FARM

The Hill County Hunt was in a profound state of shock. Two of its oldest members, one a Master and the other the daughter of one of the Hunt's founders and possibly the largest landowner, had died within six weeks of each other. The 'Hill County Hotline', as Shelley Fitzpatrick laughingly called it, had been buzzing with activity of late. However, instead of the usual gossip about who was seen driving off on a Friday afternoon with whom, this time the topic was grim. Information travels fast within every Hunt, and almost as quickly among the extended family of all other foxhunters. The specifics of Felicia Blackwell's death, following so closely behind that of Edmund Evans, were the talk of every Hunt in the southeast.

Miss Felicia's body had been found by her housekeeper on Thursday morning, lying face down on the cold grass between her barn and house, a rather sudden and inappropriate way for a grand dame to die. She appeared to have suffered a fatal heart attack, but because she had no history of heart disease, the Hill County coroner had ordered her body to be autopsied.

At first, Annabelle wondered if she would now have two ghosts to contend with, and considered that Miss Felicia would probably be more agreeable than Edmund. After a few days, however, it seemed that if Felicia had decided to appear to anyone, it wouldn't be to her. Annabelle knew Miss Felicia didn't have many living relatives. She thought there was a nephew in Maine who had dropped out of society to make pottery, and was rabidly against any form of hunting. Hunting had been Felicia's life. He was not present at her memorial service.

Most of the members of Hill County Hounds were in attendance, however, including Annabelle, Nick, and their friends the Fitzpatrick's and Robertson's. Warren Fitzpatrick spoke once again, as did Charles Collins, but there were fewer 'famous' folks than had attended Edmund's service. Annabelle reflected that Felicia had kept a much lower profile than Edmund, but, then, most people did.

Annabelle decided to have a gathering at her house after the service. She had loved and admired Felicia and felt it was the least she could do to honor her friend. The weather had again turned cold as it often does in the south in early March. Annabelle's farmhouse had been built in 1911, long before the invention of conveniences like central heating, so had a fireplace in every room. This was one of the features Annabelle loved best about her home—the fireplaces and the simple, elegant craftsman design. Today she put every hearth to good use, and as a result the interior of the house was warm and inviting.

Shelley and Marguerite volunteered to help place food on the table and to set up areas for drinks and coffee. Many of the Hunt members had brought covered dishes beforehand. As the three women reheated casseroles and stacked plates and forks within easy reach of guests, they spoke somberly about the recent tragedies.

"Funerals are getting to be a common occurrence around here," said Marguerite, putting the cups and saucers next to Annabelle's big silver coffee urn.

"I know! Can you believe it?" said Shelley. "Two of the most influential members of this Hunt have gone in a little over a month! You know, they say 'Death always come in threes'. I hope there's no truth to that old superstition. We can't afford to lose anyone else."

A chill ran down Annabelle's spine as she thought about what had almost happened to her on Wednesday.

"Well, at least Felicia got to hunt on the last day of her life," said Marguerite. "She always said she wanted to hunt as long as she possibly could."

"That's true," said Annabelle. "She was always afraid of getting sick and infirm, having to spend her last years in a rocking chair instead of on a horse. In a way, we should be happy for her."

"I suppose," said Shelley. "I sure will miss her, though. Exactly how old was Felicia? Do either of you know?"

"I don't," said Marguerite.

"Seventy-five," said a familiar, ghostly-voice close to Annabelle's ear.

"I think she was around seventy-five," Annabelle repeated dutifully. "Not too old to help me out on Wednesday," she added.

"That's right. I heard you got sick over at Waterford, said Shelley. "Charles said when everyone got back to their trailers after the hunt, Tiller told him you'd gotten overheated, or something."

"Yes. I don't really care how cold it gets, but I've never been able to hunt in warm weather." Annabelle didn't feel like going into her suspicions about being poisoned.

"I'm sure glad Tiller was grooming for you," said Shelley. "At least you didn't have to deal with taking your horse home."

"That's for sure. He was really sweet about it. He gave me a cold Coke and took great care of Samson. When I checked him later that night, Tiller had brushed him down and fed him."

"Yes, he's a very reliable fellow. Remember how disorganized poor Edmund used to be before Tiller came to work for him?"

All three ladies laughed, recalling how Edmund frequently arrived at a Meet minus some vital piece of tack, such as his girth, and very often had to borrow from someone at the last minute.

"I had more interesting things on my mind than being organized," said Edmund, obviously pleased that they were discussing him, "usually having to do with one or the other of you ladies."

Annabelle snickered, causing her friends to look at her strangely. "Just got a little choked," she said, clearing her throat and coughing slightly.

"It's a shame he was only able to work for Edmund for six months or so before he died," said Nick, who had come in to see if there was anything he could do to help.

"Yes, he needed him for years before that," said Annabelle, now apparently recovered, as she handed her husband a large platter of smoked salmon to put on the sideboard. "I'm glad Charles decided to hire him. He comes in handy around here."

Soon the other guests arrived, stomping their feet from the cold and rushing to the fireplaces to warm their hands. Annabelle noticed that while everyone had been extremely sad about Edmund's death, there had still been a lot of chatter and loud reminiscing about his many exploits. Today, however, the Hill County members behaved like a group of school children who had just been called down for talking too much. They stood around in small groups and whispered softly to each other, sighing and shaking their heads in disbelief over recent events.

Annabelle's favorite Field Master, Warren, who was known for his dapper clothing, was looking uncharacteristically somber in a charcoal wool suit as he expanded on a story he had told during the eulogy. Felicia Blackwell had been the first woman to ever win a steeplechase at the Iroquois, Nashville's grandest race meeting, riding her father's horse, Mr. Fox, in the Gentleman's Race, a competition between amateur jockeys. That part of the story was common knowledge.

"What few people know, however", Warren said, "is that Miss Felicia's father had threatened to disown her if she rode in that race, partly out of fear for her safety, but mostly because he didn't think it was proper for a woman to ride in the Gentleman's Race. He argued with her right up until she mounted. After she'd won and was the 'toast of the town', he'd conveniently forgotten he'd ever said a word against the idea."

Warren's little audience sighed and shook their heads, recalling how determined Felicia was when she had made up her mind about something. Annabelle was thinking she would have to ask Edmund for more details about this latest story when Randall Dodge appeared at the Farley's front door.

She observed him covertly for a moment as Nick took his coat. His face looked very pale and drawn as if he'd not slept the night before. On the other hand, his clothes looked as if he'd slept in them for several nights.

"Annabelle, darling!" he cried as he approached his hostess. "How are you feeling? Charles and I were so worried about you."

Annabelle stifled a shudder and forced herself to return his embrace.

"Oh, I just got too hot in my tweed coat and hunt cap," she said. "It's happened to me before on warm days."

"Well, I'm glad you're okay," said Randall, continuing to hold his arm around her shoulders. "Little did we know it was to be Felicia's last foxhunt."

"I know," said Annabelle, "and I caused her to have to come in early. She's probably cursing me somewhere right now."

"Nah," said Randall. "She wanted to help you or she wouldn't have done it. No one could ever make Felicia Blackwell do anything she didn't want to do. Maybe she was already feeling bad herself, you never know."

Something about this pierced Annabelle's consciousness. She broke away from Randall's encircling arm and went to greet other guests as they arrived, looking around for Edmund as she went. As a hostess, she had no time to analyze her feelings, but Edmund was not visibly lurking about and she was not to have a moment to herself for several hours. People felt comfortable commiserating around the many fireplaces and tended to linger. By the time the last guest departed and she and Nick had cleaned up the remains, Annabelle was too tired for introspection so went early to her bed.

- -

The next morning dawned as cold as the one before. After Nick left for work, Annabelle lost no time in dressing herself for the outdoors. An idea had come to her before rising and she wanted to act on it immediately. As she was zipping her paddock boots over her heavy woolen socks, she heard a familiar voice at her elbow.

"Where are you going so early?" Edmund asked, materializing right beside her on the window seat.

"I'm going over to Felicia's to see what I can find out. Do you want to come along?"

"Yes, of course, but what do you expect to find?"

"I really don't know, but my gut tells me to check it out. Needless to say, I don't have the greatest confidence in the abilities of the Hill County Sheriff's Department."

Edmund smiled to himself, causing Annabelle to think he had created a monster by enlisting her help as a sleuth. "So you think Felicia was the victim of foul play?" he asked indulgently.

"Yes, I do, and what's more, I think her death was connected with yours in some way."

Edmund frowned. "That doesn't add up, Annabelle. What reason would Randall Dodge have for wanting Felicia out of the way? She knew nothing about MotionTech's problems, because I was the only one he'd told. He made that rather clear."

"She may not have known about the problems, but remember, she was an investor," said Annabelle. She crossed the room to her bureau drawer where she'd put the purloined fax still hidden in the book under her silk long-johns for safe-keeping. "Look!" she said, stuffing the folded papers under Edmund's nose. "She had the most to lose—after you, of course." He took the sheets from her and read for the first time since his deadly 'accident' what Randall had sent him. Felicia Blackwell's name was on the list of investors, second only to himself in the amount she had entrusted on Randall Dodge's advice.

"That's right! I knew that!" Evan said, still flipping through the pages. "I must have just forgotten. I've been through quite a lot lately." He grinned broadly at Annabelle.

"Well, what do you think? Is Randall planning to just kill all the investors in MotionTech, or what?"

Edmund laid the fax on the seat beside him and folded his arms across his chest as he often did when considering a serious quandary—one that couldn't be answered by referring to *Beckford on Foxhounds*.

"He kept insisting that given enough time and more capital, MotionTech could still be a viable endeavor. Problem was, I wouldn't agree to throw good money after bad, nor would I encourage the other investors to do so. That was one of our chief points of disagreement. At any rate, maybe he thinks he's buying time. Felicia's estate will be tied up for months, as will my own. In the meantime, MotionTech still has the use of our funds."

"But that doesn't get him more capital to work with," said Annabelle, proud of how well she felt she was keeping up with Edmund on the investment jargon.

"No," said Edmund, "it doesn't do that. I suspect he. . ."

"Hey, what's this?" asked Annabelle, holding up another fax sheet.

Edmund waived his hand dismissively. "Oh, that has nothing to do with this. You must have picked it up by mistake."

Annabelle looked back down at what appeared to be a handwritten note. "You don't see many faxes written in longhand," she said, her curiosity suddenly aroused—"Sloppy longhand, too." She read aloud, *"Heard about your comments. Guess I'll have to wait a little longer to hunt Hill County!"* It's signed R. Davenport. Is that the same Richter Davenport who is the Master of Waterford?

"Yes," said Edmund, "he's a strange one—very anti-social. Only likes to communicate by fax even when a brief phone call would do."

"What does he mean about waiting to hunt Hill County?

Edmund's features assumed an uncharacteristically pained expression. "It's a rather unpleasant thing. As you know, Richter and his Hunt have lost almost all of their hunting territory. He and Charles are friends, and he asked Charles to try to subtly evaluate how I would feel about Davenport becoming a Joint Master of the Hill County Hounds. Naturally, I sensed what Charles was up to and told him firmly I would never back Davenport for a Mastership and would, in fact, oppose the suggestion openly if necessary. Charles apparently told Davenport what I had said and I guess he couldn't stand to let me have the last word."

Annabelle's curiosity wasn't satisfied. "Why are you so against the idea of him becoming a Joint Master? I agree he's not a very outgoing guy, but surely it's more than that."

"Actually, Davenport can be quite charming when he feels it's in his best interest. I've known him for years and our relations have always been cordial. But I've also seen how he deals with people. What's that phrase, "My way or the freeway?""

Annabelle laughed. "I think you mean "My way or the highway.""

"Yes, that's it! The Waterford Hounds were in good shape when he took over as Master, but needed an infusion of cash to repair the kennels and club-house. Davenport wooed them with extravagant tales of his hunting abilities and financial largesse, and they fell for it. As I said, he can be persuasive when he wants something. After he was made Master, not only was the cash not forthcoming, but he proceeded to alienate most of the landowners with his arrogant attitude."

Annabelle made a disgusted face. Davenport sounded like the exact opposite of Edmund who had known landowners were a Hunt's greatest asset and treated them accordingly. She listened as Edmund continued his discourse on Davenport.

116

"He also has a terrible temper when crossed, and when some of the longtime members dared to complain about the loss of their hunting country he basically told them that if they were unhappy with the way he did things they could find somewhere else to hunt—not the best way to keep members or landowners happy.   At any rate, the Masters of Hill County work well together because they are willing to compromise for the good of the Hunt.   I couldn't see us ruining that dynamic by bringing in a demagogue."

"You mean another one," said Annabelle, grinning.

"Hummph," said Edmund.   "By the way, and changing the subject, why haven't you said anything to Nick about the poison incident on Wednesday?"

"It just seemed silly to be complaining about myself after Miss Felicia died.   I'm just not ready to say anything to anyone about all of this yet.   I feel foolish claiming to be in some sort of danger.   It sounds like some hysterical bid for attention."

Edmund shrugged his shoulders.   "Well, it sounds as if you've decided not to listen to me . . . "

"I am listening to you, but I also have to listen to my own instincts."

"Choose your own path, then," he said, throwing up his hands.

"Oh, Edmund, don't be so dramatic," said Annabelle, donning her coat.   "It will all work out, you'll see.   Are you coming with me or not?"

"Might as well," he said, fading out slowly.   "I'll see you there."

Miss Felicia's estate, known as Blackwell Farm, was located on 250 acres of Guilford's finest hunting land.   While not as old as some of the Hill County residences (Felicia's father had built the house and barn in the 1920's), Blackwell

Farm was certainly one of the loveliest and best maintained properties in the hunt country. The entrance to the long drive was flanked by simple brick columns, one of which bore a concrete marker with the words, Blackwell Farm, est. 1922, carved into it. There was no gate barring the way. Guilford's crime rate was essentially zero with the exception of foxhunters exceeding the speed limits in their trucks and SUVs.

Annabelle drove up to the silent house, unimpeded. She got out of her Mercedes and quietly closed the door behind her. She would just as soon not be caught snooping around the home of yet another dead Hunt member.

"Edmund?" she asked in a low voice. "Are you here?"

"Right beside you," he said, materializing. True to form, he seemed to have forgotten he was miffed and had decided to enjoy himself. "What are we looking for?" he asked.

"I told you, I don't know. Let's see if the house is locked." Annabelle trotted up the front stairs to the wide, covered porch and put her hand on the doorknob. She tried to turn it carefully at first, then used a little more force, but to no avail. Blackwell Farm's house was clearly locked.

"Damn!" said Annabelle. She went over to one of the huge floor-to-ceiling windows and cupped her hands around her eyes, hoping to see inside. What she could see of the large sitting room was immaculate, a silent testimonial to the fastidiousness of its late proprietor. Annabelle went from window to window on the bottom floor to peer into the house's interior, each one giving the same result. The only evidence to be found was proof of Felicia's meticulous housekeeping, and nothing else.

"Let's try the barn," she said to Edmund. "After all, she was found between the house and the barn, right?"

"I believe so," said Edmund. "I still don't know what we hope to accomplish, but I must say you are quite entertaining to watch as you creep around in your Barbour coat and paddock boots like a well dressed Peeping Tom."

Annabelle rolled her eyes but made no comment, and began tromping across the lawn to the barn. To Edmund's amusement, she appeared to be looking closely at the ground like a foxhound hoping to pick up the scent of a coyote.

The big double doors to the barn were open, but the stalls were without their equine occupants.

"Wonder what happened to her horses?" asked Annabelle, as she stood in the empty barn hall.

"Tiller took them to Charles' place so he could tend to them until they are sold or claimed by her heirs," said Edmund.

"How do you know all this?" asked Annabelle in amazement.

"Just listening to the talk at your little gathering yesterday," he said with a smug smile.

"Eavesdropping, you mean." She couldn't resist teasing him.

"Whatever," he said airily, doubtless having picked up the expression from some teenaged horse groom.

Annabelle walked to the tack room. To her surprise, the doorknob turned easily and she was able to walk right in. Edmund followed, his feet touching the ground only occasionally.

Annabelle looked around the immaculate room. "There must be a fortune in saddles alone, right here," she said. And, of course, every bridle, every halter, and every single piece of leather was sparkling clean as if it had just come from the tack shop—except for one. Annabelle walked over to the cleaning rack. The saddle Felicia had used on Wednesday was already spotless, but draped across the seat was Winston's bridle, still muddy from Felicia's last hunt.

"Edmund, look at this!" cried Annabelle. "She must have been cleaning her tack just before she died."

Edmund surveyed the scene. "I believe you're right, my dear. It looks as if she had finished with the saddle and was about to start on the bridle when something must have caused her to stop."

Annabelle continued to visually examine the area. She reached out to remove the bridle intending to hang it in its proper place, but instead she drew back sharply.

"What's the matter?" asked Edmund.

"Fingerprints," said Annabelle archly.

"Oh, hell," said Edmund. "That thing is too muddy to carry a fingerprint. And, besides—what was that?"

Annabelle had turned to leave the tack room, and as she did the toe of her boot connected with an object on the ground that subsequently went sailing across the room. "I kicked something," said Annabelle, walking over to the corner where the thing had landed. The glint of metal caught her eye and she gasped. Something told her she had found the clue she was looking for.

CHAPTER XIV
THE LOCAL CONSTABULARY

"What is it?" asked Edmund, now hovering over her shoulder.

"It's Miss Felicia's flask!" She looked up at him excitedly. "Edmund, do you know what happened?"

"No, but I have a feeling you're about to tell me," he said with a grin.

"She was drinking out of this flask while she was cleaning her tack, and there was something more in it than the usual brandy!"

"You mean someone poisoned her, too?" asked Edmund.

"I mean she's the one who was *meant* to be poisoned," said Annabelle triumphantly. "She was the target all along. I only got sick because I took a couple of sips from her flask. That part was an accident."

Edmund looked doubtful. Annabelle remembered, though, how he had made negative gestures when she had drunk from the flask during the hunt.

"Look, Edmund," said Annabelle, determined to convince him. "I remember she had particularly asked Tiller to put her tack in the back of the truck so she could clean it. As soon as she dropped me off, she came in here and started to work. Then, since we didn't have a chance to drink much during the hunt—in fact, she didn't drink at all that I saw—she decided to nip on her flask while she was working on the saddle. Before she could start on the bridle, the poison hit her system and she couldn't even make it to the house and a telephone!" Annabelle was acting out her theory as she

121

described it to Edmund. "And, unlike me, she didn't throw-up after two sips. In my case, the fact that I was riding in the heat probably saved my life. My stomach couldn't take the combination of poison, heat, and jogging up and down on a horse."

Annabelle parked herself on the little wooden stool Miss Felicia had used when polishing her gear. "Surely there's some way to prove this one, Edmund." She cocked her head to one side and looked at her dead friend. "You aren't saying much. You were the one who first mentioned poison, remember?"

"Yes, I remember. I'm not saying anything because I haven't had a chance!"

"Sorry", Annabelle said, grinning sheepishly, "but I'm really excited about this. Can you blame me?"

"No, of course not," said Edmund, seating himself on a similar wooden stool, "but we have to think this through." He took a deep breath and cleared his throat. "In the first place, if Miss Felicia was poisoned, the autopsy will reveal that fact."

"I don't know. What if they used something very difficult to detect? Doctors won't be looking for poison— they'll just be checking to see if she had a heart attack. Besides, maybe some poisons cause a person to have a heart attack."

"Well, I guess that could be." Edmund sat with his arms crossed again, silently moving his mouth back and forth as if considering a topic of great importance. Finally he spoke. "I haven't wanted to involve the police in this. I haven't thought we had enough evidence to convince them. I've been afraid of making you lose your credibility."

"You didn't mind me telling Nick," Annabelle interrupted.

"That's different. He's your husband. And besides, at the time I thought your life was in danger. I can't do much to protect you, myself, anymore."

Annabelle reached out to pat his arm which was still elegantly clad in its scarlet wool sleeve that was showing a spot or two here and there. "Thank you, Edmund."

"Anyway, I think it's time the police were brought in. There's no other way to make sure Felicia's body is checked for poison."

"And," said Annabelle, rising to her feet, "that flask should be checked before the murderer realizes he needs to remove it."

"Exactly," Edmund nodded in agreement. "Why don't you tell Nick tonight?"

Annabelle raised her eyebrows at him. "I believe I'm capable of talking to the police myself," she said with a frown.

"Annabelle," said Edmund firmly, "you don't know these southern law enforcers. They're still not likely to listen to a woman. Just tell Nick everything we've discussed and let him go to the Hill County Sheriff."

"Nope!" said Annabelle, looking him in the eye. "I'm sorry you don't have confidence in me, but I'm going to the police myself, right now. By tonight, someone may have tampered with the evidence."

"Oh, for heaven's sake, Annabelle, this isn't an episode of "New Detectives"! Just wait until Nick gets home."

But, Annabelle had left the barn and had sharply shut the door behind her, allowing the flask to remain where she'd kicked it.

"You can come with me if you want to," she said over her shoulder as she headed toward the Mercedes and the Hill County Sheriff's Department.

The Hill County Sheriff's Department was in the town of Bedford, which was even smaller than Guilford. It consisted of a Sheriff who was elected by the good people of Hill County, and a Deputy hired by the former Sheriff who remained employed by his successor.

These two Officers of the Peace worked out of a small building constructed of concrete blocks which also contained the jail—one cell with some bars on its window.

There were two late-model patrol cars (the pride and joy of the County Commission), one of which was parked out front when Annabelle pulled up. It was marked with a big gold badge and the words *Hill County Sheriff's Department – Deputy* in blue letters. Not being familiar with the Sheriff or his second-in-command, Annabelle felt she had no basis for knowing whether she was in luck or not.

The metal door in front had a half-glass window suitably inscribed. She opened the door to find herself face to face with Deputy Perry Waldrop. He spit a long stream of brown liquid into a paper cup before addressing her respectfully. "Can I help you, Ma'am?"

Annabelle smiled her most engaging smile. "I hope so, Officer. I have some information to relate regarding the death of Miss Felicia Blackwell."

"Oh, yeah—the old lady—have a seat, please, Ma'am."

Annabelle sat down in the plastic chair facing his desk. She noticed he sported a blonde flat top, was a good fifty pounds overweight, and had the remnants of his breakfast in his skimpy blonde moustache. The corners of his mouth appeared to be stained with the same brown goo he had deposited in the paper cup.

Annabelle tried valiantly to hide her distaste. "Don't be judgmental," she said to herself. "Give the man a chance."

"I have reason to believe Miss Blackwell was murdered," she said, getting right to the point.

Deputy Waldrop looked at her blankly. "Murdered," he echoed, as if pronouncing the word for the first time.

"Yes—murdered," said Annabelle, beginning to feel like an actress in a bad play. "I believe Miss Blackwell was poisoned by someone who wanted to make it appear she'd had a heart attack."

Deputy Waldrop spit into his cup again and pursed his lips as if considering what he'd heard. "Doctor said it was a heart attack. Remember, she was pretty old. Why'd anyone want to kill somebody that old?"

"Well, I'm not sure about that," said Annabelle patiently, "but I do think the one performing the autopsy needs to be told to check for poison."

The Deputy shook his head negatively. "Oh, no," he said without hesitation. "We don't never get involved with the autopsy 'til after it's done. Autopsies ain't done here in Hill County, you know. They're done up at the state capitol. They'll let us know what they find. I 'spec she just had a heart attack."

Annabelle stared at him in exasperation. "Please," she said, "just come out to her barn with me. There's a flask there that I believe she was drinking out of just before she died. I bet if we check its contents there will be some evidence of poison."

"Well, I don't know," said the Deputy. "No one's said anything to us about poison."

"*I'm* telling you about the poison," said Annabelle. "Please, just at least go out there and take the flask into evidence, or whatever it is you do. Please . . . before the murderer has sense enough to realize how incriminating it is."

Deputy Waldrop continued to shake his head slowly back and forth, his face a study in disbelief with a little disinterest thrown in for good measure.

"Told you so," said Edmund in Annabelle's right ear.

"Oh, shut up!" said Annabelle loudly.

The Deputy's eyebrows shot up into his closely cropped hairline and placed both hands down on his desk in surprise. "There's no need to be rude, Ma'am," he said with a hurt tone in his voice.

At that moment the front door swung open, and in strode a man in his late fifties wearing jeans, cowboy boots and a beautiful leather vest with a gold badge pinned to it. A rather portly figure, he took one look at Annabelle and his face broke into a welcoming smile. "Hey, there," he said, as if he'd been waiting for her visit for at least several weeks.

"Who's this?" he asked his Deputy.

Without waiting for the answer, he reached out to shake Annabelle's hand and introduced himself. "Sheriff Cedric Noah", he said, firmly encasing Annabelle's fingers in his large paw. "I don't believe we've met."

CHAPTER XV
SHERIFF NOAH ON THE CASE

Cedric Noah was only a few months into his first term as Sheriff. He had won the election by a landslide despite running against the young son of a local farmer. Surprising as that sounded, if one knew all of the facts, his new post made sense.

Noah was a native of Kentucky where he'd grown up hunting, fishing, and shooting—all skills admired by Hill County voters—so even though he wasn't really a native son, he was the next best thing. Even more important was his spectacular resume. Noah had been the FBI's Special Agent in Charge of the Middle Tennessee Office for ten years until he retired at the age of fifty-five. He had chosen to retire in Hill County because of its sporting opportunities, and because he was a good friend of the former Sheriff who had served in that capacity for twenty years before deciding not to seek re-election. The other candidate never stood a chance.

Noah was enjoying his post-retirement career as a local Sheriff, but found he missed the glamour and excitement of his former career. As soon as he laid eyes on Annabelle he immediately leapt to the conclusion she was a 'damsel in distress', so perhaps the morning wouldn't be a total loss after all.

As Annabelle shook his hand a glimmer of hope flickered in her mind. Here, at last, was another chance to try convincing someone to help her. She didn't feel she'd been having much luck with the intrepid Deputy Waldrop.

"Glad to meet you, Sheriff," giving him her most winning smile. "My name is Annabelle Farley. I've come to talk to someone about the recent death of my friend, Felicia

Blackwell." She glanced over at the Deputy. "We've just been discussing my theory that she was poisoned."

Deputy Waldrop decided to speak up. "Boss, I told her the doctors thought it was a heart attack, and that we wouldn't know anything else until after the autopsy."

"Hmm, poisoned, you say? What makes you think that?" asked the Sheriff, still holding Annabelle's hand and effectively ignoring Deputy Waldrop's comment. "Come into my office and tell me about this."

Annabelle rose to her feet, extremely pleased to have found a willing audience, even if he did seem a little *too* willing.

"Sheriff, it's really imperative that you or your Deputy come out to Blackwell Farm with me as soon as possible. I'm afraid there's a vital piece of evidence that may be removed if we don't act quickly."

Sheriff Noah finally acknowledged the presence of his faithful junior officer. "Waldrop, can you hold down the fort while I go with Ms. Farley—is it Ms. or Mrs.?"

"It's Mrs." Annabelle was glad for the excuse to clarify her status. "I'm Mrs. Nick Farley."

"Oh, that's nice," said Noah, deflated only a little. "Ready, Mrs. Farley?"

Sheriff Noah held the office door open for her as they went outside. Noah continued to display his courtly manners, opening the patrol car door for Annabelle and even adjusting the seatbelt for comfort.

As they headed for Blackwell Farm, Annabelle told him details of the suspected poisoning at Waterford on Wednesday, and about finding Miss Felicia's flask on the floor of her tack room. The Sheriff appeared to be listening intently, saying, "Oh, I see," and, "Oh, really?" in all the right places.

As she was explaining about the significance of the cleaned saddle and the not-yet-cleaned bridle, she noticed a formally dressed presence in the back seat. Edmund, in his now-besmirched red tailcoat and sitting in a police car, looked as if he had been picked up for some liquor-related misdemeanor after the Hunt Ball. Annabelle suppressed a giggle. His face wore an expression of pained indignation which further added to his appearance of being under arrest. She was amused by the contrast between the two men. They were both more like characters from a movie set than actual people, but any commonality ended there. Sheriff Noah, in his jeans and fancy vest with his gold badge prominently displayed, looked like a stand-in for Heath Ledger who had put on just a little too much weight to do any action scenes. Edmund, still slim and elegant despite the grime around the edges of his colorful attire, could have been the leading man in a Merchant Ivory film.

They pulled up in front of Miss Felicia's barn where the Sheriff exited and walked around to open the door for Annabelle.

"I would question that man's intentions if I were you, Annabelle," said Edmund, leaning forward against the protective grille separating the front and back seats.

"Oh, hush-up, Jailbird," said Annabelle wickedly. "You're just mad because you were wrong about no one listening to me."

"Hmmph," said Edmund. He sat back in the seat and crossed his arms firmly. "I don't see he's been listening as much as he's been salivating," he said with a sneer. "We'll see if he actually does anything about all of this."

Annabelle accompanied Sheriff Noah up the walk toward the barn.

"She was found about here, if I recall correctly," said Noah, indicating an area on the grass less than halfway to the house.

"Oh, my," said Annabelle, the excitement of sleuthing waning as she contemplated the reality of her friend's death. She stood still for a moment. Sheriff Noah preceded her into the barn where everything was just as she had left it less than an hour earlier, with one notable exception. The pewter flask Annabelle had kicked into the corner was gone.

Sheriff Noah surveyed the tack room obligingly, hands on his hips, not realizing that a most important clue was missing.

"Sheriff, it's not here anymore," said Annabelle, who was expressing a mixture of anger and embarrassment that made her blush bright red.

"What? The flask you mentioned?" asked the Sheriff, appearing annoyingly unconvinced in Annabelle's opinion.

"Don't you see? The killer must still be around here, close! He must have realized how damning the flask would be and came here to remove it!"

"Calm down, calm down, Mrs. Farley—are you absolutely positive what you hit with your foot was a flask?"

Annabelle's frustration increased another notch. She almost told the Sheriff Edmund Evans had also seen the flask, but caught herself just in time. Instead, she took a deep breath and tried to answer him as calmly as possible. "Yes, I'm positive. A flask is something I have no difficulty recognizing." Annabelle heard Edmund snicker somewhere in the vicinity of her left ear.

Sheriff Noah smiled indulgently. "I understand, Mrs. Farley, but think about what you are saying. You found the flask, came to my office, then, during that short time while you

130

were there, someone retrieved the flask. The timing would be very coincidental, you must admit."

The Sheriff sat down on one of Miss Felicia's wooden stools as if making himself comfortable for a long siege of talking Annabelle out of her imaginary murder.

"Sheriff, I know I saw a flask—not just any flask—but the one I shared with Ms. Felicia on Wednesday. I spotted it right there," she said, pointing to the floor in front of the doorway. "If it were still here we would almost have had to step over it to get into the room. Anyone coming in here would have seen it immediately."

The Sheriff eyed Annabelle intently. "So what do you think happened, Mrs. Farley?" he asked after a moment.

Annabelle was heartened at this sign of at least temporary cooperation. She moved over to the saddle rack where a metal hook hung just above it and to the right. A clean saddle was occupying the rack, but the bridle hanging from the hook was covered in mud.

"I believe she had finished cleaning the saddle and was starting to work on the bridle when whatever she was given to drink took effect. If she'd been drinking from the flask during the entire time it took to clean this saddle, and given the thoroughness of the job, it would have been around thirty minutes."

The Sheriff stood up and looked at the half-cleaned tack. He shook his head slightly. "She could have had a heart attack and dropped the flask."

"Yes, but ..." Annabelle started to interrupt, but the Sheriff continued talking.

". . . but that doesn't mean what was in the flask caused the heart attack."

"I drank out of that flask and got sick myself, remember?" said Annabelle. "That's what made me think of poison in the first place." She left out the fact that poison was Edmund's theory, not her own. "Besides, before it was just a hunch that the flask could contain something incriminating. Now I'm sure it did."

"Why's that?" asked the Sheriff, a split-second before he realized the point Annabelle had made.

"Because someone came here and removed it," she said firmly.

This time, he didn't disagree.

CHAPTER XVI
DINNER AT FOXFIELD

Annabelle was disappointed with the outcome of her investigation of Felicia's death. Even though he had given the appearance of believing her theory, Sheriff Noah really had no evidence without the missing flask. The investigation was essentially over before it had begun. Before they parted, he had assured her he would stay alert for any information that could possibly relate to Miss Felicia, but Annabelle didn't place much faith in his continued interest unless she could turn up another clue.

As for Edmund, he was sympathetic with Annabelle's frustration. He regarded both her hunch about Miss Felicia's death and the portly Sheriff as unwelcome distractions. "Get back to proving I was murdered by Randall Dodge!" he hissed at her.

Annabelle had been so caught-up in her new hobby that she almost forgot she'd asked the Fitzpatrick's and Robertson's for dinner that evening. Edmund, who wasn't much of a shopper, disappeared while she paid a visit to the nearest large grocery chain located in Pulaski, a town in the next county. One of the few times Annabelle missed city life was when she was forced to drive thirty miles to buy more than just the most basic of items. Milk, bread, and coffee could be obtained in Guilford, but little else. The ingredients for Annabelle's gourmet creations were sometimes hard to come-by in Pulaski, as well. She had learned to compromise by substituting ingredients and growing her own fresh herbs. However, as she looked out over her herb garden, there was little still usable at that time of year. The oregano, thyme, and sage had all died-back for the winter, leaving only rosemary and savory to flavor the meal. Luckily, she had dried tarragon on hand from her last pilgrimage to Nashville.

Tonight she planned to cook one of Warren's favorite dishes—roast chicken stuffed with herbs and served with a mushroom cream sauce. Annabelle preferred to make the sauce with cremini mushrooms because of their strong flavor, but had to settle for plain button mushrooms. She would add extra tarragon to make up for their blandness.

As she trussed her small chickens and chopped herbs to place under their skin, Annabelle thought about Miss Felicia who would undoubtedly have been one of the guests tonight but for the actions of some maniac. She felt sure someone in their midst was responsible for the murders of two of her friends, and her helplessness in the matter was very frustrating. As she worked on her meal she tried to see the situation through the eyes of Sheriff Noah and the rest of the world. The two individuals had died in very different circumstances. The only certain connection between the two events was their mutual membership in the Hill County Hounds. Annabelle paused for a moment in her preparations. Perhaps she should be more worried about her own safety at this point. A small shiver of fear climbed down her backbone.

"Edmund?" she called softly.

"At your service," came the immediate reply.

"Where are you?"

"I'm right here, Annabelle." This time he materialized in his usual spot in the window seat next to the sleeping terriers which were now so used to his presence that they didn't even stir. "What's the matter?"

"Oh, nothing, I just felt a little—oh—concerned, I guess. This is serious business."

Edmund gave her a smile of understanding and amusement. "It *is* serious, as you say. I certainly never thought you would be in any danger, or I never would have solicited your help. This second murder is totally unexpected."

In an instant, Annabelle's expression changed from worried to triumphant. "Aha! So now you do think Felicia was murdered!"

Edmund rolled his eyes at the return of Annabelle's enthusiasm. "Well, I have to admit that I saw Felicia's monogrammed flask in the tack room just as you did, and someone had definitely removed it by the time you got back with the 'Rhinestone Cowboy', although I guess someone could merely have stolen the flask—it was sterling, I believe."

Annabelle made a face at Edmund. "And left thousands of dollars worth of saddles there for the taking? Not likely. Whoever killed Felicia knew it was evidence and removed it, not realizing we'd already been there and seen it."

"As much as I hate to admit it, you may be right, although that doesn't necessarily mean there's a connection between her murder and mine."

"Randall Dodge was around for both events, wasn't he?"

"I'm just trying to keep you from jumping to conclusions, my dear. We must keep our minds open—and you must promise me to be careful."

Annabelle had poured herself a glass of red wine as they talked and sat it down on the counter as if in reaction to the soberness in Edmund's voice. "I don't really know what 'careful' means in this situation. The murders are so different. I don't know what to be watching for. You'll be around to help if I'm in any real danger, right?"

Edmund looked surprised by the question and answered, "Of, course, my dear, of, course. Now, finish cooking or your reputation as a hostess will be ruined."

Annabelle grinned and reclaimed her wine glass as Edmund slowly faded back into the ether.

The Robertson's arrived around seven o'clock with a bottle of wine and a Commodores CD Annabelle had coveted when at their house a few weeks before. Nick, who preferred Mozart, knew he was outnumbered in his own home when "Brick House" started blaring from the speakers in the kitchen ceiling. Noting his resigned expression, Annabelle put her arm around him and said, "We'll compromise. I'll turn it down a little, will that be okay? This music reminds me of my ill-spent youth."

Nick laughed. "All right, I know when I'm beaten, but tomorrow night, *The Marriage of Figaro.*

"You got it," said Annabelle with a grin and handed him a fresh scotch.

Sharing the Farley's red wine and munching on various cheeses their hostess had set out for them, the two couples chatted about their favorite topics -- horses, memorable hunts from past seasons, and, of course, their fellow foxhunters.

Harold recalled an episode of a few years ago when a Hunt from Canada came to visit Hill County, bringing twenty-four hounds and as many members. The afternoon had been still and damp—perfect hunting weather. The riders of the guest Hunt were beautifully turned-out and well-mounted on eager steeds. Hill County had provided a Stirrup Cup, and afterwards everyone rode enthusiastically after the visiting pack. There is always a little pressure on both the visitors and the hosts when a Hunt visits another's territory, and this time was no exception. The visiting Huntsman cast his hounds into covert after covert, but no game emerged. After about forty-five minutes of earnest searching, the visiting First Flight Field Master had yelled "Tally-ho!" and waved his cap triumphantly.

The Huntsman quickly collected his pack and came galloping to him, blowing his horn to summon his Staff of Whippers-in with the Masters of both Hunts in tow. To their dismay, all of the excitement had been caused by a very large grey housecat that had taken one look at the hounds and prudently climbed a tree! The Field Master was embarrassed at the time, but even more-so when his mistake was commented on by the more creative members of the Hill County Hounds. The Robertson's had hosted a fabulous party after the hunt and Harold felt it only appropriate to greet each of his guests with cries of "Tabby-ho! Tabby-ho!"

The Robertson's and Farley's were laughing with the subject turning to speculation as to how Harold managed to avoid being involved in constant fights, when the Fitzpatrick's arrived—Charles Collins unexpectedly with them.

"I hope you don't mind us bringing this 'stray' we found," said Shelley, pushing Charles forward.

"Annabelle, I'm sorry to crash, but Shelley and Warren insisted you wouldn't mind."

"And I don't!" said Annabelle. Actually she was glad the evening was turning out to be so festive. "Come listen to this music Marguerite brought to me," she said, taking Charles by the arm. "By the way, to what do we owe this unexpected pleasure?"

"Well, it's not good news, I'm afraid. My housekeeper, Patsy, called me about two hours ago to tell me Tiller has disappeared. He must have gone sometime this afternoon. He'd turned the horses out this morning, but just left them in the pasture and didn't bring them in tonight to feed them! Can you believe it?"

"What makes you think he won't be back?" asked Shelley, as the group gathered around Charles.

"Patsy noticed the door to his apartment was standing open and the truck was gone. That's what got her attention in the first place, so we went inside to check it out. There's nothing left behind but junk—no clothes or other personal stuff."

"That's a shame!" said Nick. "He appeared to be so trustworthy! Everyone was glad when he went to work for you after Edmund died. What will you do about the truck?"

Charles heaved a long-suffering sigh. "I suppose I'll report it to the police as being stolen, but I may wait a few days just in case Tiller comes back." He threw up his hand in a gesture of dismissal. "That's not the worst of it. Now I've got to find someone else at such short notice. Patsy said she'd help out at the barn for a few days, but she made it clear she meant only a few. I'd hate to impose on her good will and lose a good housekeeper, too."

"We'll find you somebody," said Annabelle. She patted him on the shoulder soothingly as she went back toward the kitchen to check on the sauce. Something about Charles' situation seemed more than ordinarily curious to her, but she couldn't puzzle it out with a kitchen full of friends and a head full of wine. "I'll just think about it tomorrow," she said to herself as she inhaled the aromas of butter, mushrooms, and tarragon.

"Sounds good, Miss Scarlett," she heard a voice say, a ghostly smile hovering just above the bar.

CHAPTER XVII
A RIDING LESSON

The next morning didn't arrive for Annabelle until about ten thirty. She had slept heavily long after Nick had taken an early flight to the west coast, and decided to lie in bed a few more minutes for good measure even after she awoke. There was something she needed to do, but couldn't remember what it was. As the terriers jumped on her legs and stomach, wagging enthusiastic tails of good morning, the idea from last night came back to her, this time in detail. Without further delay, she jumped into her dressing gown and ran downstairs to brew a pot of coffee.

As soon as she stood she recognized a sad, familiar feeling. She was experiencing the after-effects of one of her dinner parties—the better the evening, the worse the headache. "Boy, we must have had a great time," she thought as she sipped her first cup of coffee. The only consolation was there was nowhere to go but up the rest of the day.

When her head cleared somewhat, Annabelle picked up the phone to dial Sheriff Noah.

"Who are you calling?" asked a loud voice at her elbow.

"Not so loud, please," she said, still dialing.

"Sorry," Edmund said in an unapologetic tone. "You still haven't told me who you're calling," he asked again, just as noisily.

"Shhh!" Annabelle whispered. The Sheriff had answered on the second ring. "Sheriff Noah, this is Annabelle Farley. We met yesterday."

"Oh, no, not him again!" said Edmund with a sneer.

"Shhh!" Annabelle said more firmly, which made her head ache. She gave Edmund a dirty look. "Thank you, Sheriff. I'm glad you remember me. I have something I think you should check out."

Edmund quieted, waiting to hear what she would say next.

"A man who worked for a friend of mine just up and disappeared, yesterday, apparently right after I'd been at Miss Felicia's barn."

"You don't know that!" said Edmund, again forgetting to keep his voice down.

"Will you SHUT UP!" said Annabelle, immediately putting her hand to her throbbing head. "Oh no, I'm okay, Sheriff—just a neighbor who dropped in uninvited." She looked pointedly at Edmund.

"Hummph," he snorted.

"Yes, anyway, Sheriff, I just wonder if this man left abruptly because he had something to do with Miss Felicia's murder." Edmund started to protest, but Annabelle put her hand across his mouth. "Well, it may not be connected, but he took a truck that didn't belong to him, as well. His name is Tiller—A. J. Tiller. I never knew what the initials stood for."

"The initials stood for Andrew Jackson, if I may be allowed to speak," said Edmund. "Although, why should I want to help you. I don't . . ."

"I seem to recall the letters standing for Andrew Jackson, Sheriff," said Annabelle. She listened to the voice in the receiver for a moment. "I know you can't arrest him for murder, but maybe he stole the flask. My neighbor suggested that might really be all there is to it." Annabelle gave Edmund a smirk. "The truck was a green Chevy pickup, a couple of years old, registered to Charles Collins at Change of Venue

Farm. Okay, thanks so much. Yes, I will. 'Bye now." She hung up the phone and sat down to her coffee.

"Well, that was pointless," said Edmund. "Tiller had nothing to do with any murder—or any theft, for that matter."

"Edmund, I know you liked him. *I* liked him. But it's too strange he walked-out on Charles right after Felicia's death driving a vehicle that doesn't belong to him, especially when everyone said he was so reliable."

"The poor man probably had some family emergency, and now you've sent the Keystone Kops after him."

"Well, if he's got a problem, maybe Sheriff Noah can help him."

"Fat chance," said Edmund, dematerializing abruptly, leaving Annabelle alone with her coffee and her headache.

By afternoon Annabelle felt better and decided to work Samson in her riding ring. She hadn't really had a chance to test her newly-found confidence in jumping since she had taken the log with Miss Felicia at Waterford.

She thought of her friend as she saddled Samson and wished she could telephone her to come over to critique her riding, make suggestions, and supply encouragement as she had on so many occasions. She also preferred not to ride alone in case of an accident, even though Samson was about as calm and quiet as a horse could be—unless it was the coin-operated variety. Still, at times like this when she really wanted to ride with a companion, Annabelle missed having her horse at a boarding stable where, in most cases, someone would be around to call 911 if something unfortunate occurred.

With as much determination as she could muster, she mounted and rode to the ring still thinking of Miss Felicia who had lived a long, eventful life and had faced challenges with resolution, but had never let bravery nor fear cloud her common sense and good judgment. She resolved to adopt a similar attitude.

She trotted Samson around the ring in each direction, first with only light contact on the reins while they both loosened and stretched their muscles. Then she asked him to yield his head and neck to the pressure of the bit coming through the reins from her hands. When a horse relaxes into this pressure from the rider, and simultaneously engages the muscles of his hindquarters, his balance and responsiveness measurably improve. This posture, called collection, was what Annabelle was striving for at a trot, and when achieved at that speed she would push Samson into a canter, hoping to maintain the same frame.

Samson had not been asked to work that hard lately so resisted by holding his nose up, out, and away from the pressure on the bit from the reins in Annabelle's hands. In response, Annabelle began to apply pressure, first on one rein and then the other, simultaneously squeezing her legs against his sides to urge him forward. She also began to make smaller circles, still at a trot, which further encouraged Samson to drop his head and yield to her hands.

In a little while, she had him trotting nicely. After a few rounds, she asked him for a canter. This time, the response was instantaneous. Samson went easily into a comfortable rocking-horse stride.

So far, so good, thought Annabelle, but now it's time to jump. She pointed Samson toward a low cross-rail they had jumped a hundred times before, and he hopped over it again without a fuss. Annabelle knew it was time for them to do more, and that the longer she brooded and worried, the harder it would become. In spite of her concern about a possible spill, she decided to quit warming-up and headed for the wooden coop she had built just in case she ever had the nerve to jump it. It had been sitting there for over a year, serving as a reminder of their untapped potential.

As she turned Samson toward the coop, she instinctively tightened her grip on the reins and raised her chin, trying to avoid the critical error of looking down at the jump that might cause her horse to stop.

"Relax," she heard a voice say, directly ahead of her. Edmund had appeared and was outside the ring leaning on the rail exactly in front of the coop. "You've got a death-grip on him. Relax, and just look where you're going until you get there."

Annabelle tried to do as he said. She ceased her exaggerated attempt not to look down, and instead looked directly at the coop as Samson slowly cantered toward it. "Now, look straight at me, Annabelle," Edmund said firmly, just as Samson came to within a couple of strides from the base of the coop. Annabelle looked up at her friend who, on this occasion, had manifested as clearly as when he had been alive. As she did so, she felt Samson gather himself underneath her and before she knew it, they were cantering safely away on the other side.

"That felt terrific!" exclaimed Annabelle, turning Samson and trotting back to where Edmund still stood. "How did it look?" she asked.

"It looked just fine. Now, turn him around and do it again!"

It was the happiest afternoon Annabelle had spent in a long time. She and Samson jumped the coop again and again, and their confidence grew with each one. Edmund smiled, praised, and directed operations. She even forgot about the recent murders in the joy of guiding a young horse to do his best. When she finally dismounted she gave Samson a pat on his sweaty brown neck and told him he had definitely earned a carrot or two.

"As much as I hate to bring up an unpleasant subject," said Edmund, walking beside them to the barn, "but since you insist on involving local law enforcement, hadn't you better give the Sheriff the fax we recovered?"

Annabelle stopped and let Samson immediately graze on the short winter grass.

"I don't want to pile too much on him just yet," she said. "He barely believes me as it is, and I'm afraid if I start talking about another murder victim in addition to Miss Felicia, he may decide I'm totally off my rocker."

Edmund laughed, and for once didn't argue with her. His acceptance made her feel happy again, as she had moments earlier after her successful ride.

Annabelle took off her riding helmet and stared hard at Edmund. She ran her hands through her short blonde hair and moved closer to the apparition she had long since begun to think of as real, and said, "Edmund, thank you so much for your help with my riding, both now and in the past. You've been great. I was so sad when I thought I would never get a chance to thank you. Now I want to try to pay you back by solving this awful crime..."

Edmund moved as to cup his hand under her chin and looked into her eyes. "Annabelle, dear, I always knew you appreciated me, and I mean that in every sense of the word..."

They both jumped when the barn telephone chose that moment to ring.

"I'd better get that," said Annabelle, pulling Samson along behind her. She grabbed the cordless phone that hung by the tack room door.

"Hello, Annabelle Farley?" asked a voice on the other end of the line.

"Oh, hello, Sheriff," said Annabelle, with a wink to Edmund over her shoulder. "How are you doing?"

"Hmmph," retorted the shade, as he settled in to listen to the conversation.

CHAPTER XVIII
ANNABELLE OFFERS TO LEND A HAND

Annabelle listened as the Sheriff described having located Charles' green pickup truck at the bus stop in Pulaski. He wasn't sure what that meant, but Tiller appeared to have left by Greyhound. He promised to continue to investigate and to keep Annabelle informed of any new developments.

"Thanks for the tip, Mrs. Farley," said the Sheriff before ending the call. "I'm really enjoying working with you!" Annabelle said, "Likewise", and hung up the phone.

"Was that Inspector Clouseau checking in?" asked Edmund, seeming to imply that the man's timing could not have been worse.

Annabelle cross-tied Samson in the aisle of the barn and began to remove his saddle. "Yes, and guess what? They found Charles' truck at the bus depot in Pulaski. I bet Tiller left it there and then departed for parts unknown—somewhere Noah can't extradite him," said Annabelle, grinning with excitement. She placed the saddle on a stall half-door for the moment. "I guess I'd better call Charles and tell him the police found his truck," she said, heading back to the telephone.

"Yes, why don't you do that," said Edmund, "and while you're on the phone, tell him you think Tiller was involved in Felicia Blackwell's murder."

Annabelle glanced at Edmund over her shoulder. "Well, there is some connection and I intend to find out what it is."

Charles didn't answer when she called him, so Annabelle left a message on his voicemail asking him to call her as soon as possible. She would decide how much to tell him once she got him on the phone. She placed Samson's bridle and saddle in the tack room.

"Don't you think the police will contact him, if they haven't already? Surely, even Sheriff Moses knows that much police procedure." Edmund remarked.

Annabelle laughed out loud. "It's *Noah*, not Moses, Edmund!" she said, shaking her head at his teasing.

"Noah—Moses—what's the difference? Why anyone like him would be named after an Old Testament prophet is beyond me."

Annabelle finally stopped laughing. "I want to talk to Charles, anyway. He might have remembered something important."

"Oh, no, I have truly created a monster with this detective business. And, of course, what happened to me has been forgotten in all of the excitement over this 'new' murder. Annabelle, we simply must get back on track."

Annabelle let him repeat his old assumptions and theories for five minutes before waving him away and headed back to the house.

Dusk was falling as Annabelle crossed the yard from the barn to her kitchen door, accompanied by the two terriers. Samson was snug in his stall, having devoured the promised carrot with relish before attacking his evening serving of oats. The month of March was almost over, spelling the end of another foxhunting season. The days were already warmer and longer than they had been just a few weeks before, and at six p.m. the sun was just beginning to set. Annabelle poured a glass of wine and thought a bit more about Felicia and the missing Tiller. Fitz and Floyd tussled playfully at her feet while fighting over a rawhide bone, and Edmund reappeared taking his accustomed seat by the window.

"Where on earth could Tiller have been headed?" asked Annabelle. "I hope Sheriff Noah had some luck checking the bus schedules."

"I can't imagine", said Edmund. "Didn't your policeman friend say he would question the bus station employees?"

"He told me that, yes—but I don't remember repeating it." Annabelle smiled. Here was yet another example of Edmund's uncanny ability to eavesdrop.

"Well, he speaks very loudly," said Edmund defensively. "Not exactly a sterling quality in a policeman."

"Never mind that—he did say he would try to find out where Tiller had gone, and he agrees with me that it appears he was running away from something."

"I just can't believe that. I found Tiller to be most trustworthy. He certainly never displayed any criminal tendencies."

Annabelle's telephone interrupted Edmund's eloquent defense of his former stable hand in mid-sentence.

"Hello, Annabelle?" asked a male voice on the other end of the line. "It's Charles. You rang?"

"Hey, Charles—thanks for calling me back."

"Well, I would have called you sooner, but the Sheriff was here with my pickup truck when I drove in."

"Oh, my goodness, where did he find it?" Annabelle asked. She decided that since she hadn't had a chance to inform Charles about Sheriff Noah's discovery of the truck, she would just as soon not mention her involvement.

"They found my truck at the bus depot in Pulaski, of all places. Looks like our friend Tiller had somewhere to go! Can you believe that? And, after he acted so pleased when I offered him a job—like he could never do enough to show his appreciation. Now he's left with no warning and the police are looking for him. Leave it to Edmund to harbor a criminal."

As Charles was so angry, Annabelle decided not to point out the fact that he had been taken-in by Tiller as well, and wondered if Edmund was listening-in as she had begun to expect. If so, he was being surprisingly quiet. Suddenly, a fresh idea occurred to her.

"Charles, I hate to interrupt, but did he leave anything behind?"

"What? Leave anything? You mean personal belongings? I don't think he had a whole lot, but the Sheriff's Deputy walked through the barn apartment. What are you getting at, Annabelle?"

"Oh, I just thought there might be some clue as to why he left or where he had gone."

"Well, the Deputy didn't seem to think so. Do you know something about Tiller's disappearance?"

Annabelle backtracked rapidly. "No, no. I'm just surprised, that's all. He seemed like such a decent guy when he was grooming for us at Waterford and everything."

"Oh, well. I guess he fooled everybody. I can't believe he didn't even let me know my horses were still out when he left. Of all the irresponsible things to do! Edmund always spoke so highly of him. . ."

It appeared that Edmund had had all he could stand without defending himself. "I can't believe he's trying to blame a dead man for his problems", his voice full of irritation at the young Master.

Annabelle stifled a giggle and let Charles continue to vent. She actually didn't blame him for being furious. She knew he was very concerned about his horses and always worried if he didn't have someone reliable to care for them while he was working in Nashville.

She got another inspiration. "Charles, listen. Don't worry about it. I'll take care of your horses next week, myself. Just try to find someone permanent as soon as you can."

"Annabelle, that's great! I'll start asking around this weekend."

"Oh, there's no huge rush. I can certainly pitch-in for a few days, at least."

"You're a peach! I'll see you at the hunt tomorrow?" Charles asked.

"You bet. 'Bye, Charles." Annabelle hung up the phone, smiling smugly at her own ingenuity.

"What are you planning, Annabelle? Since when do you volunteer to clean stalls?" asked Edmund, who had indeed listened closely to the conversation but couldn't quite make-out Annabelle's intentions.

"Just because that Deputy couldn't find anything doesn't mean there's nothing there. If I'm looking after Charles' horses, I have an excuse to look around his barn, don't I?"

"If I had a hat, I'd take it off to you. But do you really think Tiller was involved in Felicia's death? Or mine? We know he didn't kill *me*. I thought you were so sure the murders were connected."

"I still think they are, but you have a point. Tiller wouldn't have been at the Masters' Ball, that's for certain."

"Annabelle, I've told you who pushed me down those stairs, and I've even told you his motive. I think you're really 'running riot', here."

Annabelle smiled at Edmund's foxhunting euphemism. "Running riot" was a term used to describe hounds that ran after the wrong quarry, such as deer or raccoon instead of fox or coyote. She decided to reply with a quip of her own—"Just 'hark to me' for a while, Edmund."

CHAPTER XIX
BACHELOR PAD

As it turned out, Annabelle and Nick didn't hunt that Saturday. Nick was expected from the west coast on Friday night, and Annabelle was planning to pick him up at the airport around 10:00 p.m. She liked doing that when he traveled alone, and it had become a sort of tradition in their marriage. However, as airline travel had become much less reliable in recent years, that practice became more inconvenient for Annabelle. Recently, Nick's connecting flights were often delayed or cancelled, so Annabelle never left for the airport to meet him at the scheduled time without checking to see if his flight was anywhere near arriving. This time, however, even that prudent step failed to defy the inconvenience of travel in the post 9-11 world. After Annabelle arrived at the airport, she was informed that Nick's last connection out of Atlanta had been cancelled by Delta just minutes before he was to have boarded the aircraft. The next flight did not depart Hartsfield for four long hours.

Annabelle was dismayed. She had been happily anticipating their reunion and was looking forward to telling him about her successful jumping session with Samson, and, for the Farley's, 10:00 p.m. was not too late to stop for a light supper somewhere in town before heading back to Guilford. Now, all of Annabelle's plans would have to wait as Nick was not expected until 2:43 a.m. Although a disappointed Annabelle dutifully offered to wait, Nick insisted she return to Guilford. He planned to take a cab home when the plane finally arrived.

So, on Saturday, Nick slept-off his late night flight and was in no mood to hunt. The Farley's stayed home, a very rare occurrence during hunting season, and discussed recent events as they cooked a lavish breakfast, complete with the divine Bloody Mary's Nick had learned to make from Warren Fitzpatrick.

Nick predicted they wouldn't miss much hunting if they stayed home which turned out to be a correct analysis of the day. The sun was too hot, the warm easterly breeze blew constantly, and there was already too much green foliage for the scent to hold long enough for a good run. Closing Hunt was planned for next weekend. The hounds and horses, and even the riders themselves, were ready for a rest.

It was the first time the couple had had a chance to really talk in several days, what with the dinner party on Wednesday night followed by Nick's early flight the next morning. Now, as Annabelle sat back from the table stirring her Bloody Mary with the dill pickle wedge which was the recipe's secret ingredient, she recounted to Nick her discovery of the flask in Felicia's tack room and her subsequent introduction to Sheriff Noah and Deputy Waldrop. Although Nick couldn't help but laugh at her description of Noah and his tobacco-spitting side-kick, he took Annabelle's suspicions about Miss Felicia's death very seriously.

"It's horrifying to think you may have ingested poison out of her flask, even if it wasn't intended for you," Nick said. "Annabelle, I hope you're wrong about this, because if it really happened like you think it did there's a desperate, dangerous person in our midst."

"Well, if it was Tiller, at least he's left the area." The truth of Nick's comments had put a damper on her enthusiastic sleuthing. She didn't dare mention she felt there was a connection between Miss Felicia's murder and that of Edmund Evans.

"We don't know it *was* Tiller at this point. I'm so glad you've put this in the hands of the police, regardless of how comical they may be," Nick said decisively.

Annabelle nodded in agreement and was glad she had omitted mentioning her latest scheme to search Tiller's former living quarters. She saw a direct prohibition against further involvement forming on Nick's lips before he was conscious of it himself. After a moment, she prudently changed the topic to Samson's most recent brilliant performance, followed closely by a description of the terriers' most recent transgressions— thus passed a congenial breakfast in the Farley household.

Bright and early (for her) Monday morning, Annabelle headed for Charles' farm, Change of Venue, to check on his horses and to do a little snooping. Charles' horses were doing just fine. She gave grain to each, but left them in the pasture since the weather was warm and clear—the less time a horse spends in a stall, the better. She scrubbed and filled the water buckets in each stall so they would be clean and ready when she brought the horses in that evening. Last, but not least, she made sure the two huge plastic water troughs in the pasture were full to the brim.

Her legitimate business concluded, she tip-toed silently up the steps, sneaking as if she, herself, was a criminal. She told herself Charles wouldn't mind if she went anywhere on his farm and she was probably correct, but still felt a little guilty as she climbed the wooden staircase leading to the apartment A. J. Tiller had so recently vacated.

"I still don't know what you think you're going to find in there," said a voice immediately behind her on the stairs. Annabelle had been concentrating so closely on her purpose that she had forgotten about her ever present companion. Startled, she barely managed to avoid slamming her head on the top of the stairs.

"Would you please quit doing that!" she said testily, as she quietly turned the knob of the apartment door.

"Doing what?" asked Edmund cheerily, as he followed her into the sitting room.

"Yuck! What a mess!" Her pique at Edmund was eclipsed by her dismay at the revolting housekeeping of his former employee. Annabelle stood with her hands on her hips, reluctant to dive into the half-empty pizza boxes, beer cans, and other assorted filth that decorated the apartment in place of more ordinary bric-a-brac.

"I'm hardly the world's best housekeeper, but this is bad even by my standards," Annabelle said with a sneer. "Was he this messy when he worked at your farm?" she asked Edmund.

Edmund looked at her blankly for a second. "I don't know. I never visited his quarters. He took good care of me and my horses—that's all I was interested in." Edmund smiled at her distasteful expression. "You're the one who wanted to search this place, remember? I've told you he has nothing to do with any murder."

Annabelle began to move about the room, turning over food containers and magazines with the toe of her boot. "I know it's my idea, and I intend to look around." She brushed a layer of crumbs and animal hair off of the sofa and sat down. "This place could be quite cozy if it was fixed up by someone who gave a damn."

Edmund walked around the room, looking at the debris. "I agree, Annabelle," and stopped to sit beside her. "Why don't you tell Charles you'd like to stay here while you take care of his horses this week?"

Annabelle rolled her eyes and began flipping through the magazines she'd found piled on the floor. Tiller had apparently used them as a makeshift telephone-stand. An old fashioned phone with an extra long cord sat perched on top of the stack. Annabelle moved it to look through them.

"I wonder how much of this mess was actually made by our friend, the Deputy, during his investigation," said Edmund, as he looked over her shoulder.

"That's true. I hadn't thought of it, but he could be responsible for some of this disorder, although it's hard to imagine him being that thorough."

Annabelle continued to flip through the magazines that were mostly devoted to horse related subjects. "I like his choice of reading material, anyway." She picked up each copy of "The Chronicle of the Horse" and "Horse and Hound" and shook them slightly, hoping some scrap of paper or other potential clue would fall out, but nothing did.

She noticed the mailing label on one of the issues of "The Chronicle" had originally been addressed to Charles. "These would be expensive for Tiller to subscribe to," she said thoughtfully. "I guess Charles gave them to him when he was finished reading them so he wouldn't have to buy a subscription."

"I know. I gave him plenty of mine," said Edmund. "It beat leaving them lying around the house."

Annabelle continued to look at the mailing labels. "Yes, here's one with your name on it, Edmund." They smiled at each other. Annabelle had become so used to Edmund in spirit form that she almost felt puzzled when confronted with evidence of his former existence.

At that moment, Annabelle's cell phone rang. She looked down at the display that showed the incoming telephone number. "It's the Sheriff", and quickly flipped open the receiver, thankful for the technology that allowed Sheriff Noah to call her without knowing she was snooping around behind his Deputy.

"Mrs. Farley?" asked the Sheriff. Annabelle could tell by his voice that he had something he thought would be of interest to share with her.

"Yes, hello, Sheriff," she said expectantly.

"Are you sitting down?" Noah was really enjoying this part of his official duties.

"As a matter of fact, I am. What's up?" Annabelle couldn't help grinning at her new friend's enthusiasm.

"We've spoken with individuals working at the bus depot on the day Mr. Tiller left town. Of course we haven't confirmed it for sure, but it appears our friend took the bus to Atlanta."

Annabelle knew what that meant and her excitement fizzled. "Home of the world's busiest airport," she said dejectedly. "He could be half-way around the world by now."

"That's true," agreed the Sheriff, "but it's pretty easy to trace airline passengers these days, although it may be a little hard to justify going to that much trouble to find a man suspected of 'unauthorized use of a vehicle', which has since been recovered, I might add."

Annabelle, who had been pacing around the messy room, disappointedly sat back down again. "Oh, Sheriff, can't you use your old FBI contacts to help us? You know there's more to this than a temporarily stolen truck."

"I'm beginning to think you're right about that, Mrs. Farley, but the link between Mr. Tiller and any serious crime is just too tenuous at this point."

"Oh, well. Thanks for your help, anyway."

"Don't lose heart. Maybe something else will turn up. I'll keep in touch." The Sheriff rang off.

"Dead end?" asked Edmund, who, of course, had expected nothing else from the Sheriff.

"I'm afraid so. They think he went to Atlanta, which means he could have flown anywhere in the world."

In a dispirited fashion, Annabelle continued her perusal of Tiller's old magazines. "Edmund, did Tiller have any family or close friends in Atlanta?" she asked after a moment.

"I think it's certainly possible that Atlanta was his destination rather than just a point of departure, but I don't know of any connections he had with the place."

"Where *is* his family?" Annabelle asked, now intrigued by this new line of thought.

"What difference does that make? I can't remember offhand. I don't really know," Edmund replied, a curious expression on his face, as if he'd only just considered Tiller might have had a family.

"You certainly didn't know much about him, did you?" asked Annabelle, more in the tone of a statement rather than a question.

She was about to suggest they leave the apartment—the clutter and the smell were getting noxious—and her recent talk with the Sheriff hadn't done much for her spirits.

With a sigh, she turned over the last issue in the stack. A familiar, but unexpected, name appeared. "Edmund, where did you get Tiller?" she asked excitedly.

"Where did I *get* him? He was highly recommended to me by a friend and I hired him, if that's what you mean."

"Who recommended him?" she asked, clutching the magazine.

Annabelle handed Edmund an old issue of "Horse and Hound" and pointed to the mailing label. "Was it him?" she asked, indicating the name of the magazine's original recipient. The expression on Edmund's face was all the answer she needed.

CHAPTER XX
BUSTED

Edmund, who had been pacing about the cramped and messy little apartment while listening to Annabelle and marveling at Tiller's lack of housekeeping skills, pretended at first not to understand what she was insinuating.

"Oh, I remember now," he said, continuing to walk around. "My friend, Richter Davenport, recommended him to me. You know Davenport, don't you, the Master of the Waterford Hounds?"

Annabelle stared hard at Edmund for a moment. "I'll bet he knows where Tiller is. I'm going to call the Sheriff!"

Edmund stopped his pacing and sat down on the sofa beside Annabelle after first moving aside an old pizza box. Edmund was at least as conscious of his formal clothing in death as he always was in life, perhaps more so now since he was unable to change his attire.

"Annabelle," he said firmly but quietly, like a parent trying hard not to lose patience with a recalcitrant child, "you really must promise me you will not involve someone of Mr. Davenport's stature in these wild theories."

Annabelle crossed her arms and said nothing for a moment.

"You weren't concerned about Randall Dodge—and he is certainly a person of 'stature' as you say," she said finally.

Edmund shook his head in disagreement. "He is in his own way, but Davenport is a Master of Foxhounds and has been for years. Do you understand what that means, Annabelle?"

"I thought I did, but I have a feeling I'm about to hear an entirely different view on the matter."

"Well, to be a Master is not only the greatest honor society can bestow," he began, ignoring Annabelle's comment, "but it's an honor that carries with it tremendous responsibility."

"Kind of like being President of the United States?" asked Annabelle.

"I'm perfectly serious about this. I've listened to enough of your hair-brained theories . . ."

"Okay, okay! Go on."

Edmund took a deep breath and began again. "A Master of Foxhounds must put hunting above every other pursuit in his life. He must safely show sport to a group of individuals with widely varied riding abilities. He must court new landowners and pacify existing ones. When subscriptions fall-short he must be ready to make up the difference from his own personal funds, even if it means a hardship on himself or his family. All of this must be accomplished with a gracious attitude that makes the sacrifices appear effortless."

Edmund paused for a moment, whether for effect or simply to catch his breath. Annabelle wasn't sure.

"I say all of this to make one point—no Master of Foxhounds would risk his reputation and that of his Hunt by being involved in some petty criminal activity, the likes of which I can tell you are about to begin by accusing Mr. Davenport."

"I thought you didn't even like him that well," Annabelle said lamely.

"We don't always get along, that's true, but I've known him since he was a boy and I refuse to allow you to involve him in this mess about Tiller."

"I merely thought he might know where the man went, that's all," said Annabelle, wondering how he had managed to make her feel so guilty.

"I can see your devious little mind is working better than you realize. You think you've found some clue here, don't you?"

Annabelle pursed her lips and kept silent. She knew when she was beaten. "All right, I won't tell the Sheriff about it—just now, anyway."

"You'd better not," said Edmund, standing and brushing any possible crumbs from his coat. "I'll know if you do," he said, taking Annabelle's arm. "Let's get out of this place. I'm starting to get depressed."

"Me, too," said Annabelle sadly, thinking of her commitment to Charles which had now lost much of its appeal.

Annabelle turned over and placed the pillow more firmly against her ear. Who was calling at this rude hour? After four loud rings, the answering machine picked up the call.

"Thank goodness," said Annabelle, and turned over, snuggling down in the deliciously soft white pillows.

"Annabelle!" Charles' voice came over the machine. "If you're there, pick up! The man who delivers . . ."

Annabelle snatched up the phone with a grimace. She had forgotten her added responsibility entirely, but there was no reason for Charles to know it.

"Hello, Charles!" she said, trying to force her voice to sound alert and cheerful. "I'm sorry I couldn't make it to the phone in time."

"Annabelle, please, I know you were asleep. It's only eight-thirty and I know you never get up this early unless Nick insists you go cubbing! Annabelle made a face. "Okay, so what? If you knew I was asleep, why are you calling now?" she asked in a sickly-sweet voice.

"Because, you've got to get over to my barn as soon as possible. I know it's a pain, but I just got a call from the man who delivers my wood shavings. He's on his way and you'll need to let him through the gate."

Annabelle sat up and began to try to clear her head. Many barns use soft wood shavings as bedding in each horse's stall. She had noticed yesterday that Charles' shaving pile was getting low, but with the weather so pleasant she had been able to leave the horses outside. The early spring weather could change at any moment, however, so it was very important that the clean bedding be available.

"I'll get over there right now," she said, obligingly, while putting her feet on the floor and looking about for yesterday's blue jeans.

"Thanks, girl! I hate to ask you to do this, but . . ."

"No, I offered to help and this is part of running a barn. I need to get up anyway," she lied.

"I'm afraid there's one more thing."

"What's that?" Annabelle sat back down on the bed, one leg in her blue jeans and one out. She had that 'Oh, no' feeling.

"Tiller liked to park the horse trailer in front of the shavings pile because he said it helped keep them dry—out of the weather, you know? So you'll have to move it before the man can dump the load of shavings."

Annabelle sighed. "I haven't driven a gooseneck trailer in years."

"All you have to do is move it a few feet. It'll be all right."

"Okay. It's your truck and trailer I'm worried about. I'll give it a try, though."

After a few more words of thanks and encouragement, Charles rang off leaving Annabelle to throw on her paddock boots, a sweatshirt, and her Barbour coat, and went flying out the front door. The terriers begged to accompany her, or at least given dog biscuits as an alternative, but their Mistress had no time for either indulgence.

As she started her car she heard a familiar voice from the direction of the passenger side of the vehicle. "Poor Kiddo— gets herself in such difficult situations—all in the name of hunches, theories, and clues!"

Annabelle growled at him. "It's too early for disembodied voices," she said. "If you're going to talk to me at this hour, would you please materialize?"

In a moment, Edmund was visibly lounging in the passenger seat of the Mercedes which Annabelle had to push back as far as it would go to accommodate his long legs. "Cheer up!" he said, obviously very cheerful himself and fully enjoying Annabelle's discomfiture. "It's really not that early, you know."

"I know that," said Annabelle, still not smiling. "It would have been fine if I'd had more notice. I'm also not looking forward to trying to move that horse trailer."

Annabelle didn't bother to explain to Edmund where they were going or what trailer she referred to, guessing correctly that he had invisibly eavesdropped on her conversation with Charles.

"Oh, that's right," he said sympathetically. "Your trailer is a bumper-pull, isn't it? Have you ever driven a gooseneck rig before?"

"Yes, but it's been a few years. In fact, I can't remember the last time." Annabelle searched her memory as she drove down the quiet back roads to Charles' farm.

"Well, I'll help you anyway," said Edmund kindly. "We won't have any trouble." He patted her thigh reassuringly.

"Good," was all she replied. She was not much of a conversationalist before her morning coffee.

When they reached Change of Venue, Edmund waited in the car while Annabelle opened the big gates which she left wide for the shavings delivery man. When they got up to the barn, Annabelle jumped out and went over to examine Charles' beautiful three-horse trailer with a dressing room that was indeed parked in front of the shaving pile with only about six feet in-between.

"I see why he does this. It probably does help keep the shavings dry, but it seems like a great deal of trouble."

"I suppose so," said Edmund, who could not recall ever moving his own shavings and had no idea how they were kept dry. Edmund's wealth had assured that such tasks were always performed by someone else.

Annabelle climbed into Charles' big, green, dual-wheel pickup truck he used to pull the trailer, the same one Tiller had 'borrowed' to get to the bus station in Pulaski. Charles had thoughtfully left the key in the ignition and the big engine turned over smoothly.

"Now what?" she asked Edmund, who had clambered in beside her.

He looked at her blankly. "You just back it up under the trailer hitch, I believe."

"I thought you said you were going to help?" Annabelle was not in the mood for jokes.

"I *am* helping." said Edmund, eyebrows raised in surprise. "I'm right here, aren't I?"

"Edmund, do you know how to do this or not? Because I definitely don't. In fact, now that I think about it, I've driven one of these things but I've never actually hooked it up to a trailer."

Edmund gave her a condescending little smile. "Why don't I get out and flag you back?" he asked, wondering to himself whether or not it would actually hurt if she slapped him.

"All right," said Annabelle, getting more frustrated by the moment. She had rolled down the window and was looking back expectantly, waiting for his instructions. Edmund stood beside the trailer that had a long metal column which would attach to the hitch in the bed of the pickup truck. He knew, essentially, how the two things should connect—the problem lay in getting them to meet. He took a deep breath and tried to size up the distance between the pickup and the trailer.

"Well, first," he said in what he hoped was an authoritative tone, "you're way too far to the left. Move forward and then straighten up." Edmund gestured widely with his left arm.

"What? Do you want me to move to the left or to the right? You're pointing to the left!"

"Oh, so I am!" said Edmund quickly. "You're too far left, so you need to move to your right!" This time, he pointed in the appropriate direction.

Annabelle put the truck in a forward gear and pointed the front end to the right. Then she attempted to straighten the vehicle as Edmund had indicated.

"No, no, no!" cried Edmund, trotting up to the window but keeping out of range of Annabelle's fingers. "You're not straight! The end of the truck is angled too far to the right!"

Annabelle pulled forward, much farther away.

Using the correct arm this time, Edmund proceeded to slowly flag her back toward the trailer. "Come on, very good!" motioning with his arm and thinking how easy it really was.

Annabelle continued to ease the truck backward, seemingly in a direct line with the metal column of the trailer hitch.

Suddenly Edmund shouted, "Stop! Stop!" as they both heard the sickening rasp of metal against metal. "I said stop!" he cried, trotting quickly up to the driver's side door.

"What the hell was that?" asked Annabelle, her voice low with fury.

"You forgot to lower the tailgate on the truck so it collided with the column on the trailer!" said Edmund breathlessly.

"I *FORGOT?*" Annabelle was speaking louder by the second. She leaned as far out of the truck as she could reach. "You have no clue how to do this, do you? I'll bet you've never hooked-up a truck to a trailer in your entire life! You'd better stay back!" she said, noting that Edmund was maintaining a careful distance from the truck, just out of reach of her hands. "Of all the stupid . . ."

At that moment she became aware of another presence—one who was respectfully clearing his throat in order to get her attention.

"Oh, hello," said Annabelle, her face turning crimson. "You must be here to deliver the shavings."

"Yes, Ma'am, I sure am. Would you like a little help moving the trailer?"

Annabelle smiled gratefully at the man. "I sure would!" she exclaimed, climbing quickly out of the driver's seat.

Her rescuer was an overall-clad gentleman in early middle age with a kind face and rough hands. He gave Annabelle a sympathetic look as he took the wheel of the pickup. "You ought not to be so hard on yourself, Ma'am. Lots of people have trouble with these things. It don't mean you're stupid."

Annabelle thanked the man who expertly backed the truck to the trailer and connected the hitch. Edmund had disappeared again, but not before Annabelle heard him laughing.

CHAPTER XXI
THE LAND DOWN UNDER

Now that she was up and about, Annabelle enjoyed the mild morning weather. She fed and watered Charles' three horses while her new friend from the sawmill dumped the giant load of shavings. He introduced himself as Ned Owens, and after Annabelle thanked him profusely for helping her hook up and move the trailer, he very kindly offered to move it back into place and unhooked the hitch in case Annabelle needed to use the truck.

As Annabelle signed his receipt acknowledging delivery of the shavings, she noticed Ned had pushed his ball cap back and wiped the perspiration from his forehead with an old handkerchief.

"Can you believe it's already this warm?" she asked, as she returned his clipboard and pen. She had long since shed her Barbour.

Ned shook his head. "Sure looks like an early spring to me—'course, it could change at any minute. The last time I made a delivery here, it was so cold Tiller had to break the ice on the buckets before he watered the horses! Have ya'll heard anything from that old boy?"

It was a second before Annabelle realized Ned was referring to the missing A. J. Tiller. She tried not to betray her excitement by answering him as casually as possible. "No, we sure haven't. Have you?"

Ned grinned at her. "Naw, not me, but then I would hardly expect a call all the way from Australia."

"Australia!" This time Annabelle couldn't hide her surprise. "Is that where he went?"

Ned's eyebrows shot up. "That's what I reckon. He always talked about going down there to work for some Hunt—said the Master was a friend of the man he used to work for."

Annabelle was almost speechless with excitement over this bit of information, but didn't want to act in a way that would make Ned uncomfortable. She forced herself to react calmly. "Well, actually, he left here without giving notice. That's why I'm here pitching in temporarily," she said in what she hoped was an off-handed manner.

Ned frowned at her for a moment. "That's too bad," he said. "That old . . . ! I sort of wondered if you were the new barn help!" he said, all smiling.

They laughed again over Annabelle's inept attempt to hook up the trailer. Then Ned Owens drove away, presumably back to the sawmill for another load, but not before Annabelle noted the name and phone number of the business. She ran to the car to write down the information and then used her cell phone to dial Sheriff Noah.

"Hello, Deputy," she said when Waldrop answered the Sheriff's phone. "This is Annabelle Farley. Is the Sheriff available? Thanks, I'll wait."

"What are you doing now?" asked Edmund, who had appeared in the passenger seat.

Annabelle put her hand over the receiver. "I'm going to tell him what I just found out from that Mr. Owens," she said, with no doubt in her mind Edmund had been present and listening for the past half-hour.

Edmund rolled his eyes and stuck out his lower lip. "I really wish you would drop this idea of Tiller being a suspect and get back to our investigation of Randall Dodge. This is getting a bit ridiculous."

"Hello, Sheriff!" said Annabelle excitedly, while putting her finger to her lips and looking daggers at Edmund. "I spoke to someone today who may have some information about A. J. Tiller. He had an idea he went to Australia, and he also knows who he might be working for down there."

Edmund could hear Sheriff Noah speaking excitedly through Annabelle's cell phone.

"No, I don't know the man's name, but my informant says he's a friend of Tiller's previous employer, Richter Davenport."

At this, Edmund threw up his hands and made as if to take the cell phone from Annabelle's hand before he remembered his ghostly limitations. Annabelle moved quickly out of his reach, anyway.

"Yes, I can meet you for coffee. In fact, I haven't had my usual cup this morning." she said, trying to ignore the fuming apparition in the passenger seat. "Sure, "The Tennessean" is fine. I'll be right there." Annabelle closed her flip-phone with a click and turned to Edmund. "What on earth are you upset about?" she asked. "This is a great breakthrough in the case!"

"What case?" Edmund asked. She had never seen him so furious, living or dead. "Not *my* case. And I believe you promised not to involve Richter Davenport in all this."

Too late, Annabelle remembered she had indeed made such a vow. "But Edmund, that was before we heard Ned Owens say Tiller was working for one of Richter's friends!" She felt badly now, even though she still believed she was doing what she ought to do. "Besides," she said, trying to placate her angry friend, "if Davenport hasn't any connection with the murders, it won't do any harm to mention his name to the local Sheriff."

Edmund shook his head at her, his disappointment clearly portrayed in every feature of his face. Then he sniffed decisively and proceeded to disappear.

The Tennessean Truck Stop is a local landmark with a regional reputation. Many a cross-country truck driver has planned his route to make his mealtime stop to conveniently include the "The Trucker's Breakfast." This delicacy, which consists of hash browns, bacon, and cheddar, is a famous favorite not only of the visiting drivers, but of the locals, including the Hill County foxhunters.

On a Friday night before a Saturday hunt Meet, it was very typical to see city types down from Nashville dining beside the truck drivers and local farmers. The fried chicken was superb, and the country fried steak even better. And, for those watching their waistlines there were home-cooked vegetables of every variety (liberally seasoned with pork fat, however.)

This was not a place to overindulge in alcohol. Each customer was only allowed three beers—not enough to have much of an effect upon any of the Tennessean's usual clientele as all had a similar high tolerance for alcohol.

When Annabelle pulled into the parking lot on the morning of the meeting with Sheriff Noah, beer was certainly the last thing on her mind. It was now eleven o'clock, and she had had neither breakfast nor the all-important cup of coffee before heading to Charles' farm. She had already made up her mind not to wait on the Sheriff before ordering, but such a breach of etiquette was not necessary as he was already waiting for her at a sunny booth by the window from which he eagerly arose as soon as he saw her enter the restaurant.

172

"Hello there, Mrs. Farley," he said, rushing to shake her hand and see her settle on the other side of the booth. Today, the Sheriff was sporting a black felt cowboy hat that went with his boots, along with a stiffly starched plaid shirt embroidered with the name of a famous hunting outfitter. Annabelle smiled at him, surprised to find herself genuinely glad, or at least amused, to see him again.

The waitress appeared almost immediately. She was familiar with both of her customers, but had never seen them dine together before. She asked no questions, being acquainted with the Sheriff's penchant for attractive females. She was a little surprised seeing Mrs. Farley with him, but there was no accounting for tastes.

After she departed to the kitchen in search of coffee for two and an order of "The Trucker's Breakfast" for Annabelle, the Sheriff got around to asking Annabelle what she'd found out.

"Well, it came about completely unexpectedly," she said, now able to share her excitement with a willing listener. "I've been helping Charles Collins take care of his horses at Change of Venue since Tiller left him, and this morning I had to be there to accept a delivery of wood shavings—for stall bedding, you know." Annabelle added the last phrase by way of explanation since she had no idea if the Sheriff was at all familiar with barns and horses. She declined to mention her misadventure in moving Charles' trailer, thinking it would add little relevance to the tale. "After he dumped the shavings and was about to leave, the man from the sawmill, Ned Owens was his name, asked if we'd heard from Tiller."

Annabelle stopped to accept the much-needed cup of coffee from the waitress and then leaned forward conspiratorially before telling the Sheriff the rest of her news. "I said "no" to his question and asked if he'd heard anything, himself. He said he really didn't expect Tiller to write him from *Australia*."

The Sheriff sat back abruptly, whether truly surprised or just indulging Annabelle, it was impossible to say. "What made him think he'd gone to Australia?"

"Well, he said Tiller had always talked about going there to work for a foxhunt. He didn't know the name, but said there was some connection with Tiller's former employer."

"You mean the man that died earlier this year? What was his name—Edgar?"

Annabelle had to suppress a laugh, but sobered quickly. She hadn't considered the possibility that Owens might have been referring to Edmund, not Davenport. And she'd been too busy arguing with Edmund to ask if he knew of any foxhunts in Australia.

"The man I think you mean is Edmund Evans. But frankly, I sort of assumed Owens was talking about Tiller's employer before Mr. Evans, a man named Richter Davenport."

Sheriff Noah considered Annabelle's new information and sipped his coffee for a moment. So far, it appeared that A. J. Tiller had temporarily used his employer's truck as transportation to Pulaski where he'd caught a Greyhound bus for Atlanta. There was nothing to connect the man with any other crime, and the owner of the truck wasn't interested in pressing charges. On the other hand, Annabelle Farley wasn't going to let up on him until he did something to prove her suspicions one way or another. And, he thought to himself with pride, it was not as if he didn't have plenty of favors to call in from his many years with the Bureau. He looked across the Formica table at Annabelle's big, shining eyes and decided he had certainly risked more for less.

"I'll tell you what, Mrs. Farley," he said with a magnanimous air. "I didn't feel it was appropriate or even feasible to try to track Mr. Tiller from Atlanta to points unknown, but now that we have at least a possible destination, I'll try to find out if he went to Australia. Shouldn't be too hard with all the security checkpoints he would have had to go through these days."

Annabelle had to stop herself from jumping up from the booth and hugging the man. "Oh, thank you, Sheriff!" she said. "I just know we'll find him, and then . . ."

"And then, maybe not much, Mrs. Farley. I can't promise you we can do anything else. And if he didn't go to Australia after all . . ."

"I understand," said Annabelle, thinking she would worry about the next move when it needed to be made, but not now. She could hardly wait to hear what Edmund would say! Then she remembered something. "What about Richter Davenport? Are you going to talk to him, too?"

Sheriff Noah put up his hand in a restraining motion saying, "One thing at a time, Mrs. Farley. Let's just check out your Australian theory first."

Annabelle fought back the urge to argue and tried to be pleased with the victory at hand.

"In the meantime, I think I'll ask the county commission to let me hire you on as Guilford's number one detective," said the Sheriff.

Annabelle laughed. "I think I'll keep my amateur status for now, but please do keep me posted on the investigation."

"You bet'cha," said the Sheriff, as Annabelle's breakfast arrived and she settled back to enjoy it, unable to recall when she'd last felt so pleased with herself.

CHAPTER XXII
THE SHERIFF COMES THROUGH

To Annabelle's surprise, the week wore on without the visits from Edmund that had recently become a part of everyday life. Charles quickly hired a new groom to replace Tiller. That was just fine with Annabelle, who didn't mind helping a friend, but wasn't particularly anxious to care for another barn full of horses in addition to her own.

The Wednesday hunt was uneventful with only one brief run all day. At the tailgate afterward the hunters had to admit to each other that the season was coming to a close. Foxhunting is a cold weather sport, and the winter that had seen the passing of Edmund Evans and Felicia Blackwell was essentially over. All that remained was the upcoming Closing Hunt that was often little more than a memorial gesture commemorating the season's sport.

Annabelle, as usual, visited fellow-hunters by wandering from one chatty group to another, some of whom she would rarely see during the spring and summer months. With her ears open for clues as always, she overheard Charles mention he had extended an invitation to Richter Davenport to ride with him as his guest in the Closing Hunt. Annabelle looked forward to a chance to observe the visiting Master whom she now suspected had knowledge of at least one murder.

And, although she initially adopted a cavalier attitude toward Edmund's disappearance as the days passed and he continued to absent himself, she began to feel genuine remorse about the manner in which they had parted. She hated to think she had disappointed her friend when he had come to her for assistance. She also missed his companionship, despite his tendency to appear unannounced and cause her to spill her wine or trip down stairs. Her feeling of loneliness led

Annabelle to another level of introspection. Was it wise to be so attached to what might very well be a figment of her imagination? Even though Edmund had been materializing before her very eyes for several months, just a few days without seeing him caused her to doubt she had ever really seen him at all.

Annabelle had always been loath to give up anything to which she had formed an attachment, be it a person, an idea, or, when a child, even a favorite toy. And, there was no doubt she had been attached to Edmund Evans and looked to him for guidance as she navigated the often treacherous social seas in the world of foxhunting.

Now, as she attempted to analyze herself, she wondered if her defiance of Edmund on the subject of Richter Davenport had been a symbolic effort to chart her own course, independent of his counsel. The trouble was, Annabelle felt far less confident now that he was no longer around for her to disagree with. She continued to consider various theories about the murders, and actually came up with several interesting scenarios. Unfortunately, Edmund hadn't reappeared to listen to them. So, Annabelle looked forward to observing Richter Davenport's behavior at the Closing Hunt and waited to hear from Sheriff Noah about his investigation of A. J. Tiller's whereabouts. There didn't seem to be much else she could do.

- -

After a week that Annabelle felt had lasted several months, Friday evening finally arrived. It was the night before Hill County Hounds planned to hold their annual Closing Hunt and Guilford was buzzing with activity. All of the foxhunters were in town, including some that only hunted a few times each season.

The Closing Hunt Tea would be held at Shelley and Warren Fitzpatrick's farm where Annabelle and Marguerite had been helping with the preparations most of the day. If Annabelle was any good as a prognosticator of how a party would turn out (and, of course, she was an expert on the subject), this one promised to be a genuine blow-out. Warren was a connoisseur of dance bands and had chosen one of the very best in a town full of great bands to come down from Nashville for the afternoon. Shelley had hired a huge tent to shade them from the now ever-present southern sunshine and filled it with delicious foods and two bars serving premium liquors.

As glum and introspective as Annabelle had been all week, she began to cheer up considerably at the prospect of such a good time. She also determined to stick to Richter Davenport like glue, despite his legendary inapproachability. She went to the barn to braid the horses' manes in a cheerful frame of mind.

As she stood on a stool to reach the top of Samson's big draft head, Nick came to the barn carrying two generous glasses of red wine with the bottle tucked under his arm. He reached up to kiss her and they laughed at the disparity in their heights, which was usually the other way around.

"The Fitzpatrick's and the Robertson's are on their way over," said Nick, sitting down in a chair and holding Annabelle's wine for her as she worked. Braiding a horse's mane is definitely a job requiring both hands.

"Just to hang out?" asked Annabelle, pleased.

"Yes. Their horses are already braided and they said they would come entertain you since you were so slow."

Annabelle laughed, and a few moments later she heard a truck pull up outside the barn, followed by Harold Robertson's infectious laugh. He bounced in with a cocktail and looked

178

critically at Samson's half-braided mane. "Good grief! What a head of hair that horse has got!" he said critically.

"You obviously haven't told him 'big hair' went out in the 80's," added Marguerite.

No one could resist teasing Annabelle about her beloved horse, if only to hear her insist, for the hundredth time, that he was perfect in every way. Annabelle took the bait, knowing she would disappoint them if she did otherwise. "Samson is proud of his draft-horse roots, and so am I," she said with her nose in the air.

"Well, he certainly has enough of them," said Harold, quickly taking advantage of the opening Annabelle had given him.

The three couples laughed and chatted while Annabelle finished Samson's mane, then she stepped down from the footstool to work on his equally generous tail. She was just tying-off the end of the braid when the barn telephone rang.

"I'll get it," said Nick, who had been feeling slightly guilty watching his wife at work. In a second, he stuck his head around the tack room door and said in a mock whisper, "It's for you, Annabelle. It's the Sheriff."

A collective 'ooh' rose from the assembled foxhunters, who giggled and taunted their friend. "What have you done now, Annabelle, more 'breaking and entering'?" asked Warren with grin.

Annabelle wiped her hands on an old rag and went to the phone, inwardly cursing Charles Collins and his big mouth. When she heard Sheriff Noah's news, however, all thoughts of her friends and their teasing were forgotten. She couldn't help but be impressed with the Sheriff's FBI connections this time.

"Mrs. Farley," he said breathlessly, "I hate to bother you so late, but I thought you'd want to know as soon as possible.

We've confirmed that Mr. Tiller did, indeed, fly from Atlanta to Melbourne, Australia, but not before he was forced by air security screeners to leave something very important behind."

"What on earth?" asked Annabelle, trying to keep her voice low.

"A monogrammed sterling silver flask." replied the Sheriff.

CHAPTER XXIII
CLOSING HUNT

Annabelle slept very little that night. The fact that Miss Felicia's flask had been in the possession of A. J. Tiller when he'd left the county had finally given Sheriff Noah the probable cause he needed to make her death the subject of a possible murder investigation with Tiller the prime suspect, but locating him in Australia might be difficult or impossible. And besides, Annabelle still felt sure a major piece of the Edmund/Felicia puzzle was eluding her. She had told the Sheriff all she knew about Tiller's connection with Davenport and hoped he would see fit to question him. She'd even let him know that Davenport was expected at Guilford the next day for the Closing Hunt.

Her mind worked in circles around Tiller, Edmund Evans, Randall Dodge, and Richter Davenport. Annabelle had no doubt there was some connection between Miss Felicia's death and Tiller's obliging help on that lady's last hunt. And, there was even less of a question in her mind regarding Tiller's past and present link to Davenport. However, she was still left with pieces that didn't appear to fit into the picture, anywhere. It certainly seemed as if Randall Dodge had murdered Edmund—Edmund himself was sure of it. He had both motive and opportunity. Perhaps the two deaths were unrelated other than by coincidence, but every time Annabelle's thoughts reached that point she felt more positive she was missing some key piece of information. She would turn over and make one more effort to go to sleep, but within minutes she was back again like a confused foxhound with too many coyotes to chase. Each time the scent led back to where it had begun, with the original game getting cleanly away.

When morning finally came Annabelle awakened groggily, somewhat surprised to realize she must have slept at least a few hours. Despite the lack of sufficient rest, excitement soon took over and she was wide awake, full of nervous energy once more. She dressed in record time and grabbed a bagel on the way out of the kitchen door to the barn. Samson and King were pacing in their stalls as if sensing their braided manes and tails meant today would be special. Closing Hunt was always held in the morning, in hopes that enough scent would linger for the hounds to work despite the warming weather and greening grasses. Annabelle was glad for once, and felt she couldn't have stood waiting until afternoon.

Soon the Farley's were hauling their horses to the Meet with Annabelle chatting nervously all the way. Nick assumed his wife was excited about the last hunt of the season and the party at the Fitzpatrick's afterward, which was certainly true. Annabelle had mentioned her suspicions about Richter Davenport to no one but Edmund who still refused to show himself.

Like all 'High Holy Days', the Closing Hunt of the Hill County Hounds was always well attended. Although the Farley's were by no means late for the Meet, dozens of horse trailers were already lined up in triple rows along the Fitzpatrick's fence line. As trailers full of riders turned into the gated entrance, the occupants were greeted by Warren and Shelley who offered cups of port or brandy.

"Make mine a double," said Annabelle to Warren with a sheepish grin.

"Annabelle, you better stay on top of your horse today," he answered back, but still honored her request for an extra libation.

Annabelle quickly downed the contents of her glass and handed it back to Shelley who was collecting empties.

"I feel better already," she said, only half in jest, and Nick pulled the trailer into the pasture to find a suitable place to unload the horses.

As Annabelle put finishing touches on Samson's tack and gave her boots a final polish, she looked around for Charles whom she assumed would be accompanied by Richter Davenport. Soon she spied Charles' trailer several rows down on the left. His new groom was working to ready two horses that were tied to the trailer, but there was no sign of either of the young Masters. Annabelle was peering so intently down the row that she nearly jumped out of her skin when Charles hailed her from the opposite direction.

"Sorry, Annabelle!" he said, laughing at her obvious surprise. "I didn't mean to scare you. You're nervous as the old coyote himself, this morning."

Annabelle smiled, remembering the night he had caught her at Edmund's house looking for clues.

"You remember Richter, of course," Charles gesturing toward the visiting Master who was standing a little behind him.

"Of course," said Annabelle, turning to smile at Richter. In spite of her suspicions, Annabelle forced herself to look him full in the face. He merely touched his hunt cap coldly at her in response, clearly not interested in making small-talk, even with a Master's wife.

"We need to talk to Nick about today's plans. Is he around?" asked Charles.

"He should be in the dressing room on the other side of the trailer," answered Annabelle, still looking at Richter Davenport despite his cool reception.

As the two young men made their way to look for her husband, Annabelle stopped smiling. "I'll find a way to talk to you today whether you like it or not," she thought grimly to herself.

The Meet was scheduled to start promptly at 9:00 although, as usual, a few latecomers had to be accommodated. The Masters welcomed everyone and hoped for a good day's sport, and just before the Huntsman turned to trot away with the pack, Warren asked for a moment of silence.

"Let's pause a moment to remember our late Master, Edmund Evans," he said, removing his hunt cap and holding it against his heart. "This is Hill County's first Closing Hunt without him in over thirty years," he said quietly. "May his spirit be with us today!"

"Amen!" said the other Masters. Everyone lowered their eyes for a few moments except Annabelle who looked up without raising her head in a covert-attempt to gauge the reaction of the Master of the Waterford Hounds. As usual, his face was an inscrutable mask as he replaced his hunt cap and prepared to ride off at Charles' side.

Annabelle took her place just behind Warren at the head of the Second Flight. She toyed with the idea of moving up to First. She looked at Samson's ears that were pricked forward, interested but not worried, and felt he seemed capable of doing whatever she asked. But, since Davenport would be riding somewhere with Charles and possibly not with the First Flight anyway, it seemed pointless to change. She was slightly disappointed in herself for this was her last chance of the season. But, as she had told herself before, this was hardly her last season to hunt and she would feel it when the time came to take that first coop.

Warren led them at a brisk, comfortable trot through the woods and Annabelle looked around her at the budding trees. The Tennessee hills were donning their spring wardrobe even as the hunt chased the last of winter down the curving, rocky path.   Annabelle could hear the soft voices of her fellow hunters behind her, chatting and laughing irreverently as they would never have done when the weather was cool and a hard run was anticipated around every corner.   Then the hounds struck for a brief time and all talking ceased as the surprised hunters settled in for a gallop, but very soon the hounds were quiet again, having lost the scent after a few moments in the rapidly warming air.

The Second Flight made their way out of the woods and down onto one of the few paved roads in the Hill County territory.   Although pavement was by no means the preferred footing for foxhunting—the Hunt threw up its collective hands every time another road was 'ruined' by the County Commission—Annabelle liked to hear the sound of trotting hooves as they clattered down the blacktop.

Her earlier nervousness now past, she listened to this peculiar music and forgot everything else momentarily.   She was just thinking how she would miss this particular sound over the summer when she noticed the Hill County Sheriff's car moving slowly down the road ahead of the hunt.   She could see Sheriff Noah's broad form inside and her previous excitement returned in an instant.   The Sheriff braked the car as soon as he saw riders in his rearview mirror.   Annabelle waved a brief acknowledgement to Warren who made no attempt to hide his surprise when she trotted past him to the Sheriff's car. She jumped to the ground and leaned into the open window, holding Samson's reins in one hand.

"Hello, Mrs. Farley!" said Sheriff Noah, heartily.   "I'm sure glad we found you guys! Didn't you tell me that fellow Richter Davenport is out here today?"

Annabelle could hardly believe her ears.   "Yes, Sheriff, he's riding up ahead with one of the other Masters."

"Well, we need to take him in for questioning. You were right about Tiller. As soon as we mentioned Davenport he knew we had him. Squealed like a stuck pig—and guess who he claims put him up to it? Davenport!"

CHAPTER XXIV
FIRST FLIGHT

Annabelle felt her heart constrict with a strange dread now that her hypothesis seemed proven correct, at last. She tried to hold Samson close to Sheriff Noah's police car, her labored breathing causing him to pull away slightly as he sensed some fear in his rider.

"Mrs. Farley, if Davenport is here today, I'd like to take him in for questioning."

Annabelle snapped out of her reverie and urged Samson back to the car window. "He's here, Sheriff, probably with the First Flight."

Sheriff Noah made no reply for a moment. He had no idea what she meant by First Flight, but he did know what he needed from Mrs. Farley right now. "Could you point him out to me? The man doesn't seem to like to be photographed." "And I would never recognize anybody in this foxhunting 'get up', anyway, the Sheriff thought to himself.

Annabelle turned and cantered back to Warren, who was still holding the Second Flight group on the paved road.

"Warren, where is First Flight right now?" asked Annabelle, breathlessly, as she pulled Samson to a halt beside him.

"They're not far ahead of us on the road, right in front of the cross-roads by the Masterson farm. Billy is drawing that good covert to the left. Why? What on earth is going on, Annabelle?"

Annabelle saw her friend's worried expression and smiled what she hoped was a reassuring one. "I'm just helping the police with something minor. I'll be right back," she said over her shoulder as she cantered back to Sheriff Noah.

"What?" called Warren after her, his usual quiet and dignified manner for once deserting him.

Annabelle didn't answer. She cantered as fast as she dared on the paved roadway—something she had rarely done with Samson because of the danger to both horse and rider presented by the hard, slick surface. Samson's initial surprise at his rider's change in attitude had by now turned to excitement. He stopped reluctantly this time, dancing a little beside the open window of the police car.

"If he's still with Charles Collins, then they're somewhere close to First Flight up ahead."

"I need you to point him out to me, Mrs. Farley," said the Sheriff.

"I can lead you to there, Sheriff, but I'm not sure he'll be with them." There was no way Annabelle would volunteer to try to track down riders like Collins and Davenport.

"Just do what you can. I'd like to interview this guy before he finds out we've got Tiller. With his money, he could go practically anywhere in the world in a matter of just a few hours."

They agreed that Annabelle would trot casually up to First Flight as if she were simply joining them at a 'check', then try to approach Davenport and ride beside him long enough for Sheriff Noah to pick him out of the crowd. Noah would give Annabelle a few minutes, and then he'd pull in behind the riders as if he were conducting his normal patrol of the area and needed the hunters to move over to let his vehicle pass.

As Annabelle trotted away from the Sheriff and the security of Warren and Second Flight, she found herself wishing for Edmund's counsel and encouragement. As many times as she had envisioned the day when she would finally ride Samson in First Flight, she had never dreamed of a circumstance like this. In recent months, her plans had always included having Edmund nearby. She had only a moment to wonder, yet again, about his disappearance before she saw those bringing up the rear in First Flight just ahead of her with the rest of the group out of sight around the curve of the road.

"Hey, it's Annabelle!" said one of the hunters before being 'shushed' by a more prudent comrade. Foxhunters are expected to wait quietly while the hounds search a covert for game so as not to distract them from their work.

"Hey, girl, you joining us?" asked the same friendly hunter, this time in a lower tone.

"I thought I might," said Annabelle, trying to seem as matter-of-fact as she could manage. "By the way, have you seen Charles and Richter Davenport lately?"

The rider, who was removing his flask from its leather holder in order to show Annabelle a bit of First Flight hospitality, answered immediately, "Oh, yes. Charles has been leading the Flight and Davenport has 'stayed in his pocket' the whole time. They're right up there around the corner," he gestured. "Liquid courage?" he offered with a smile.

If you only knew, thought Annabelle, taking the flask and drinking a quick, but serious, swallow. "Thanks," she said, wiping her mouth with her glove. "I've got to get a message to someone," she added as she began to weave her way to the front. She was immensely relieved that Davenport was not off beyond her reach.

Annabelle tried to make her approach quietly, but her many friends had to greet her and whisper their congratulations and approval of her decision in joining them. About half of them passed their flasks into her hand, and both good manners and good acting dictated her acceptance of each one. Nothing would arouse suspicion quite like Annabelle refusing a drink. It took far longer than she had expected for her to reach the front of the group, but when she finally did she saw Davenport sitting on his horse next to Charles, a little away from the rest as he usually seemed to prefer.

Her rather dramatic progress to the head of the line had not failed to arouse the attention of the leaders and both men turned to look at Annabelle as she walked Samson toward them—Charles with a welcoming smile and Davenport with boredom and annoyance.

Charles rode forward a few steps to meet her. "Well, Annabelle! I'm so glad you've come up to join us at last. Samson will do fine. You just stay right behind Richter and me. We'll help her, won't we, Rich?" He turned to grin at Davenport. "You know, Annabelle's really a good rider, but I was beginning to think she'd never ride up here with me. Now, today, she finally decides . . ."

There was some movement in the rear of the group. As Charles was speaking the sound of a car engine could be heard on the road. " 'Ware car," said Charles to his Flight as the Sheriff's car came slowly into view.

Annabelle's eyes went immediately to Davenport. He had flinched ever-so-slightly when he saw the police car come around the bend, but, otherwise, his inscrutable face betrayed no emotion until he caught Annabelle's eye and saw that she was watching him. Although she tried to look away, the intensity of his gaze held her spellbound. As many times as they had met, Annabelle had never felt Davenport's attention focused in her direction until now. The look in his eyes was one of such utter hatred and cruelty that instinctively she began to back Samson away. In the next instant, Davenport turned his thoroughbred and, giving it a firm slap on the rump, disappeared off of the road and into the woods.

CHAPTER XXV
THE HUNTER BECOMES THE PREY

It was a long moment before someone reacted. To the surprise of both the foxhunters and Sheriff Noah, that 'someone' was Annabelle Farley. Giving a kick to Samson like he'd never felt before, she turned the big horse on a dime and galloped into the woods after Richter Davenport.

The hateful, warning look Davenport had given her pierced Annabelle's heart and had proven to her, more eloquently than clues or evidence ever could, that this was the man who had taken the life of her dear friend. She knew in that split-second when he dashed into the covert that she would never forgive herself if she sat prudently on her horse, ruled by fear and self-interest, and let Edmund's killer get away.

Now, as the branches tore at her Melton jacket and scratched her velvet cap, Annabelle sat her hips down in the saddle and leaned her head and shoulders along Samson's neck. She had glimpsed the back of Davenport's scarlet coat for a mere second, so leapt into the woods after giving Samson another firm kick that sent him hard after the other horse. Never was Annabelle more grateful for his willingness to obey her without argument.

Despite Davenport's big head start, Samson's huge strides put them in sight of the thoroughbred in just a few seconds. When Annabelle saw the scarlet coat within some one hundred yards, she gave him an encouraging cluck and growled to him, "Come on, boy!" The horse responded by giving her a burst of speed, understanding now that he was chasing the horse in front of him. Not imagining himself pursued, Davenport had pulled out of the thick covert and onto one of the rocky trails used by the Hill County Hounds. Samson's huge hooves slipped on the limestone imbedded in the path and he sat back on his haunches to balance himself down a shallow incline.

Unfortunately, Annabelle's cry of encouragement had alerted Davenport to her presence. He glanced quickly over his shoulder—not too quickly for Annabelle to note the look of surprise followed by a disdainful sneer as he recognized his pursuer. He didn't bother to increase his already considerable pace, but headed for the end of the woodland path and out into an open field.

Annabelle knew the Guilford country and realized that Davenport was heading for a stretch of open pasture where his thoroughbred could quickly outdistance a heavier horse. She rose slightly in the stirrups to take as much of her weight off of Samson's back as possible, and struck him firmly behind her leg with the end of the hunt crop she still clutched in her hand. The startled Samson shot forward out of the woods and into the pasture, almost unseating Annabelle who scrambled to regain her balance. She could still see Davenport ahead, halfway across the big field. Suddenly, he turned sharply to the left and it was as if he disappeared into the very earth.

Samson was now following Davenport without need of much guidance from Annabelle, and he immediately began cutting to the left to shorten the distance between himself and the other horse. As he did, Annabelle remembered where they were and realized what had caused Davenport to vanish from view. They were almost to a steep drop-off that even the boldest riders avoided.

She felt herself instantly cold and sweating in her Melton, her hands slick with perspiration beneath her thin, white gloves. She wanted desperately to pull Samson back from the crest, but was equally afraid of interfering with his balance. She sat back in the saddle, putting her feet far forward and lengthening her reins, trying to stay out of her horse's mouth and help steady him as much as she could. Samson didn't hesitate, and engaged his huge haunches to propel them quickly down the slope. His naturally careful nature was vying with his instinct to run and catch up with the horse ahead of him. As a compromise, he slowed down only slightly as they followed Davenport.

Annabelle fought the urge to close her eyes and then wished she hadn't. Davenport had flown fearlessly down at a full gallop and she immediately saw what looked like a gigantic coop at the foot of the hill. Davenport never slowed his mount, but flew effortlessly over and out of sight.

When Davenport disappeared yet again, Samson increased his pace in an attempt to keep the other horse in view. Annabelle was terrified. In the few seconds it took for Samson to collect and approach the jump, a hundred thoughts passed through her mind, none of them happy. "Should I try to pull him up, or would that do more harm than good at this point? What if he stopped at the bottom of the coop?" Given the speed at which they were approaching it, there was no way she would be able to maintain her seat. She imagined herself thrown head-first over the coop onto the pavement. "Pavement?" To her horror, she saw that the jump's landing was almost directly onto a roadway.

In reality, Annabelle grabbed a handful of Samson's generous mane and held on for dear life with both legs. As for Samson, he didn't even consider stopping at the coop. He merely patted the ground lightly on takeoff and used his big hindquarters to power them smoothly over to the other side. He landed squarely on the pavement, skidding only slightly for a moment before lunging forward into a gallop after Richter Davenport. Annabelle's heart felt as if it would burst from relief, pride, and renewed determination. She sat deep in the saddle and urged Samson on, not caring now if Davenport or anyone else heard her voice.

The fleeing Master had not stayed on the paved road for more than a few seconds and had turned back into the safety of the woods. He glanced back at Annabelle only once, as if surprised she had managed to follow, though still unconcerned, much like an experienced coyote judging the relative danger of a particular pack of hounds.

He led Annabelle over coop after coop and, despite losing her stirrups over one more difficult, she continued to pursue him closely. With survival now her chief goal she had little time to think of the consequences of actually catching Davenport. They were galloping along the edge of a steep ravine, Samson scrambling to stay on his feet as they slid over rock after rock. Annabelle saw he was having much more difficulty than he'd had at the beginning of their chase, and realized to her dismay that he was starting to tire.

She was proud of him. Nothing in their experience together had remotely prepared him for such a run, yet he had handled the stress like an old pro. But, now he was winded. His sides and chest were covered with lather, and the reins were soggy from the perspiration of both horse and rider.

Then, it seemed to Annabelle that Davenport, too, was slowing. The distance between them diminished until she was only a few horse lengths behind him. He whirled to face her, holding his dancing, straining thoroughbred on a tight rein. "All right, you stupid bitch, here I am. What do you want from me?"

Annabelle's initial shock at being confronted by her prey quickly gave way to the anger she had felt at the beginning of the chase. "You killed Edmund Evans!" she practically spat the words at Davenport.

"So what if I did!" said Davenport, now moving his horse forward toward Annabelle. "You're a fool to interfere in my business!"

In a flash, Davenport pulled alongside Samson and struck him violently across the flanks with his hunting crop. Samson darted forward and sideways, his back feet scrambling for purchase on the edge of the ravine. For a few seconds it felt as if he would surely slip backwards down the precipice, but he used his massive shoulders and neck to pull himself back onto the path. Annabelle shifted her weight forward in the saddle to help him regain his balance, and took off at a gallop away from Davenport.

She didn't get far. Davenport had a faster mount, was much the superior rider, and was buoyed by the confidence of a killer who had killed before. He easily caught up with Samson and began to shove his horse into Samson's shoulder, forcing him to the left and off the edge of the path. Samson tried to lunge forward, away from the other horse, but when he did, his left front hoof slipped across a rock in the path and he went down on his nose. Annabelle fell forward onto his neck which pulled him further off balance, and as he attempted to right himself, she felt the reins jerked out of her hands.

She forced herself to look at Davenport's face one last time. It was all there—annoyance, cruelty, hatred, even pride in what he was about to accomplish. Now holding her horse's reins, he pushed Samson backward toward the edge of the path, only a few feet to the edge of the ravine. Samson, tired as he was, leaned his giant body away from it, but Davenport raised his hands so that the horse's head was pushed up in the air, using the weight of his head and shoulders against him. Samson's back feet dug into the edge of the precipice.

Later, Annabelle would try many times to relate what happened in those next few moments and always said the hardest thing to describe was the uncanny stillness that seemed to descend on the forest. Seconds before, the striking of the horses' hooves and the grunts of their struggles had mixed with other woodland noises, filling the air with sounds. But, suddenly, the forest had become quiet as a grave.

Annabelle saw the blood leave Davenport's face as he dropped Samson's reins. She still had one hand clutching a handful of mane as she struggled to regain control of her horse. Only when she had the reins securely back in her own hands did she look up to see what had startled Davenport.

On the path, not ten feet away, stood Edmund Evans in his scarlet attire, solid and real as ever he was in life. Davenport made a strangled sound and yanked his horse brutally backward away from the apparition.

Edmund approached him purposefully with one hand raised in a gesture that could be either a threat or blessing, his face a study in grim determination.

Annabelle watched transfixed as Edmund pressed the frightened horse and rider closer and closer to the precipice. Davenport's face was frozen in a grimace of terror, his arrogance for once deserting him. Edmund lifted his hand toward the horse's bridle, and when he did, the frightened thoroughbred reared on its hind legs and pawed at him with its front feet, rolling his eyes like a mad thing. The horse's hooves passed right through Edmund's body. As solid as he appeared, here was proof of his existence only as a spirit.

Finding his pawing to no avail the horse reared again and, to Annabelle's astonishment, threw Davenport off of his back and sent him tumbling toward the rocky chasm.

Annabelle sat limply on her tired horse. Edmund stepped back from the edge and gave Annabelle a wide, triumphant smile. Then, he slowly disappeared.

CHAPTER XXVI
MASTERS BALL

By the time Nick and Charles located Annabelle, curiosity had mastered fear and fatigue. She had dismounted and crept carefully to the edge of the ravine. Holding Samson's reins, she peered over the side of the bluff to discover the fate of Richter Davenport. She could see a limp form wearing a scarlet coat about halfway down the steep descent, his fall appearing to have been broken by one of the huge hardwood trees growing on the slope. Opinions would differ as to whether the tree's intervention was a good or a bad thing for Davenport. Although it very probably saved his life by keeping him safe from the rocks below, the blow to his head apparently affected his brain in a permanent fashion. Forever afterward he would claim he had been forced off of the cliff by Edmund Evans who, as everyone knew, had been dead for three months.

Apart from these delusions, Davenport was amazingly unhurt, suffering only a broken arm despite having taken a fall that could certainly have killed him. In fact, he regained consciousness as he was being loaded onto the stretcher by the emergency medical crew. A Med-Flight helicopter had been dispatched as soon as Charles called 911 on his cell phone, and Davenport had begun mumbling about Edmund Evans to anyone who would listen—the doctors, Charles, even Annabelle who promptly refused medical attention if it involved being transported in the same helicopter with "that murderer".

It would take several weeks for Sheriff Noah to discover all of the connections between the two murders and he lost no time in communicating the sordid story to Annabelle. When he found out Davenport's motive, his belief that foxhunters were crazy was thoroughly reinforced. But Annabelle, understanding foxhunting as she did, was not particularly surprised.

Andrew Tiller had been more than willing to 'rat out' his old boss in return for a reduced punishment for his part in the murder of Felicia Blackwell. According to Tiller, Davenport and the Waterford Hounds had fallen victim to a foxhunter's greatest enemy—the land developer. Their hunt country had been slowly eroded by housing subdivisions. Davenport's arrogant attitude had done little to endear him or his hounds to the local landowners, and some had sold their property just to thwart him.

Edmund Evans' charm had made the Hill County territory safe from encroaching development, and their 40,000 acres of game-filled hills were too much of a temptation for Davenport. He installed Tiller to work for Edmund with the mission to find out about Hill County's arrangements with its landowners, willing to purchase the territory if necessary. However, Tiller's observations confirmed that as long as Edmund was alive, no landowner in the Hill County hunt country would dream of selling to an outside Master.

So, Davenport booked a room at the Pierre Hotel on the night of the Masters Ball knowing Edmund would be in attendance. He hadn't dressed for the Ball, himself, and no one had noticed an ordinary looking tourist among the peacocks in scarlet. He waited until Edmund was alone and gave him a powerful shove down the famous staircase.

With Edmund and his influence out of the way, Davenport had then set about attempting to purchase Hill County territory from the largest landowner in the area— Felicia Blackwell. It took only a vague illusion to realize she wasn't about to sell, so he dropped the subject before anyone could become suspicious. He then took the next logical step of contacting her nephew and heir who was far more receptive to

Davenport's offer. In fact, he agreed to sell all 10,000 acres to him as soon as he inherited. Davenport then used Tiller's proximity to Felicia to shorten the old lady's life.

In return for this information, the prosecution agreed not to seek the death penalty in Tiller's case. His lawyers considered this a victory under the circumstances, and he pled guilty to one count of murder and received a sentence of life in prison.

As for Davenport, he was indicted on a long list of charges that included first degree murder, conspiracy to commit murder, and solicitation of murder. However, his continued insistence that he had been attacked by Edmund Evans, and his unshakable belief that Evans would again "try to come back for him" at some point, made an insanity plea a natural choice for his defense attorney. He was committed permanently to a state institution for the criminally insane, a fate of which he had no argument as long as his caretakers promised to protect him from Edmund Evans.

As for Annabelle Farley and the Hill County Hounds, both continued their pursuit of coyotes, uninterrupted. Charles Collins approached Felicia's nephew about purchasing the land that was now his in Hill County, and within a month following Davenport's arrest he was not only the youngest Master of Hill County Hounds, but also its largest landholder. He further distinguished himself by placing the entire parcel in an irrevocable trust so that it would never be developed, ensuring enjoyment by foxhunters for generations to come.

Annabelle was never able to explain her involvement in the whole matter to anyone's satisfaction, so she uncharacteristically avoided the limelight when she could have legitimately claimed the status of 'heroine', at last. Despite her successful cross-country pursuit of Davenport, she continued to ride with the Second Flight the following season, confident she could jump as high and gallop as fast as anyone in the hunt field, but trusted Warren Fitzpatrick's hunting expertise to put her consistently in the best spot to view a coyote.

When Edmund Evans' ghostly form did not appear again, Annabelle assumed his mission to find his killer had been accomplished and he had gone on to hunt with Ronnie Wallace, the Duke of Beaufort, and other great departed foxhunters. In fact, when the date of the Masters' Ball rolled around again, Annabelle had almost convinced herself Edmund had never appeared at all.

This year, New York City was not as cold as it had been the night of Annabelle's first Masters Ball and the ladies *almost* agreed to walk the short distance from the Plaza to the Pierre Hotel alongside their husbands. They had only traveled a few feet down the sidewalk of 57th Street when Annabelle spotted the now-famous rickshaw and stopped to flag down the driver.

"Come on, girls!" she said with a grin. "It's tradition!"

With much protest, Marguerite and Shelley followed their friend into the weird little conveyance, and to the amusement of their husbands, were whisked away to the Pierre by the struggling driver.

The Pierre had lost none of its glamour during the previous year. In fact, its penthouse apartment had recently sold for over $70 million. As Annabelle looked about the fabulous lobby she wished for a moment that she could live there herself, but quickly dismissed the idea when she realized that Samson and the terriers would have no place to run.

As the three couples crossed in front of the fateful staircase, Annabelle tightly squeezed her eyes shut for a moment. She was determined to shed no tears that night. She had done all she could for Edmund and, wherever he was, he knew he had never had a truer friend on either side of the firmament.

"Would you look at that?" said Shelley, interrupting Annabelle's noble thoughts. "I'm proud for Edmund! Don't you know he would love being immortalized at the Pierre!

The little group stopped at the bottom of the staircase. The powers-that-be at the hotel had installed a discreet brass plaque on the banister at the foot of the stairs where Edmund had died. It was tastefully engraved with the words, "In memory of Edmund Jay Evans, 1936 – 2003".

"That's lovely," said Marguerite, her head bowed respectfully as she read the engraving. Then she looked up and grinned mischievously. "Who knew he was that old?" she asked. And the group moved off into the dining area, discussing their old friend's amazing ability to hide his age all those years.

The Hill County group located their assigned seating, and then paired off to the dance floor. Annabelle looked up at the chairs where officials of the MFHA were seated, along with their spouses. If Nick Farley continued to distinguish himself as he had done in recent months, there would no doubt come the day when Annabelle would find herself among that elite company. She should have been pleased by the idea, and she was, but she couldn't deny that something was missing.

She danced with one of her favorite partners, Charles Collins, who spun and twirled her across the floor in such a professional manner that other couples stopped dancing and stepped aside to watch them. After he dipped her almost to the floor in a finale, the crowd clapped and the band announced their first break. Charles and Annabelle stood together for a moment, catching their breath.

"Thanks for the dance, Annabelle," said Charles, patting her shoulder.

"Thank *you*—you know I love dancing."

"Yes, I do know," said Charles, "but you don't seem your usual cheerful-self tonight."

Annabelle looked down, embarrassed that her attempt at gaiety had been such an obvious failure. "It's just that none of this seems quite right without Edmund."

Charles shook his head sympathetically and tucked Annabelle's arm beneath his own, preparing to escort her from the dance floor. "I know he meant a great deal to you, Annabelle. We all miss him, but life goes on. Think of all you have to look forward to this spring. The racing season is almost here—in fact, it's time we began planning the Iroquois."

"The Iroquois? Edmund was a big part that race for so many years! Planning it without him will just make me miss him more."

"Oh, Annabelle, you've got to snap out of this! Edmund lived a full life and now he's gone on to another. It's not right for you to keep feeling this way."

Annabelle listened half-heartedly, knowing he was only trying to help her. He couldn't possibly understand that while everyone else had had a year to get used to life without Edmund Evans, she'd had only had a few months! She was about to thank him again for the dance and make her way back to the table when she glimpsed a familiar sight out of the corner of her eye. She stood frozen for a moment, causing Charles to pull away from her as he continued to walk.

"Annabelle?" his voice full of concern when he realized she had stopped. "Are you all right?"

Annabelle was staring at one of the mirrored columns that lined the dance floor of the Pierre. Casually leaning against it with his arms crossed over his chest was the tall, elegant figure of Edmund Evans dressed in white tie and scarlet tailcoat. He gave Annabelle a broad grin and a long, slow wink.

"Yes, Charles," said Annabelle, recovering her composure and looking up at him with her happiest smile, "I think everything is just fine."

Acknowledgments

There are several people without whom the writing and publishing of this book would never have been a reality. The first who comes to mind is my friend and former paralegal, Lisa Bullock, who painstakingly typed the original document from longhand and even claimed to enjoy it. The second is my riding instructor, Ken Keister, who introduced me to foxhunting and then taught me how to stay alive while enjoying my new sport.

Another is Andrea Garrett, my first foxhunting buddy and fellow literary enthusiast, whose encouragement and friendship has helped me in so many areas of my life, of which writing is only one.

I also owe a debt of gratitude to Henry Hooker, MFH, who introduced me to foxhunting in the hills of Tennessee and was the first reader of the completed manuscript of The Masters Ball. If he hadn't given my scribbles a good review, you wouldn't be reading this now.

Many thanks to Larry and Jerry Pefferly for believing in me and pushing me to get this project completed and for Jerry's invaluable help in editing the final product, and to the great Poppy Hall for her priceless artwork.

And finally, much love and thanks to Albert Menefee III and his beautiful wife, my dear friend Theresa, for the best foxhunting "home" a hunter could wish for – The Cedar Knob Hounds!

CPSIA information can be obtained at www.ICGtesting.com
Printed in the USA
BVOW021644220412

288245BV00001B/7/P